The Great God Success

The Great God Success

A NOVEL

By

JOHN GRAHAM
(DAVID GRAHAM PHILLIPS)

THE GREGG PRESS / RIDGEWOOD, N. J.

First published in 1901 by Grosset & Dunlap
Republished in 1967 by
The Gregg Press Incorporated
171 East Ridgewood Avenue
Ridgewood, New Jersey, U.S.A.

Library of Congress Catalog Card Number: 67-29277

Printed in United States of America

AMERICANS
IN
FICTION

INTRODUCTION BY PROFESSOR CLARENCE GOHDES

Editor of *American Literature* Magazine

In the domain of literature the play may once have been the chief abstract and chronicle of the times, but during the nineteenth and twentieth centuries the novel has usurped the chief place in holding the mirror up to the homely face of society. On this account, if for no other, the Gregg Press series of reprints of American fiction merits the attention of all students of Americana and of librarians interested in building up adequate collections dealing with the social and literary history of the United States. Most of the three score and ten novels or volumes of short stories included in the series enjoyed considerable fame in their day but have been so long out of print as to be virtually unobtainable in the original editions.

Included in the list are works by writers not presently fashionable in critical circles — but nevertheless well known to literary historians — among them Joel Chandler Harris, Harriet Beecher Stowe, Thomas Bailey Aldrich, and William Gilmore Simms. A substantial element in the list consists of authors who are known especially for their graphic portrayal of a particular American setting, such as Gertrude Atherton (California), Arlo Bates (Boston), Alice Brown (New England), Edward Eggleston (Indiana), Mary Wilkins Freeman (New England), Henry B. Fuller (Chicago), Richard M. Johnston (Georgia), James Lane Allen (Kentucky), Mary N. Murfree (Tennessee), and Thomas Nelson Page (Virginia). There is even a novel by Frederic Remington, one of the most popular painters of the Western cowboy and Indian — and another, an impressive minor classic on the early mining region of Colorado, from the pen of Mary Hallock Foote. The professional student of American literature will rejoice in the opportunity afforded by the collection to extend his reading of fiction belonging to what is called the "local-color movement" — a major current in the development of the national belles-lettres.

Among the titles in the series are also a number of famous historical novels. Silas Weir Mitchell's *Hugh Wynne* is one of the best fictional treatments of the American Revolution. John Esten Cooke is the foremost Southern writer of his day who dealt with the Civil War. The two books by Thomas Dixon are among the most famous novels on the Reconstruction Era, with sensational disclosures of the original Ku Klux Klan in action. They supplied the grist for the first great movie "spectacular" — *"The Birth of a Nation* (1915).

Paul Leicester Ford's *The Honorable Peter Stirling* is justly ranked among the top American novels which portray American politics in action — a subject illuminated by other novelists in the Gregg list — A. H. Lewis, Frances H. Burnett, and Alice Brown, for example. Economic problems are forcefully put before the reader in works by Aldrich, Mrs. Freeman, and John Hay, whose novels illustrate the ominous concern over the early battles between labor and capital. From the sweatshops of Eastern cities in which newly arrived immigrants toiled for pittances, to the Western mining camps where the laborers packed revolvers, the working class of the times enters into various other stories in the Gregg list. The capitalist class, also, comes in for attention, with an account of a struggle for the ownership of a railroad in Samuel Merwin's *The Short-Line War* and with the devastating documentation of the foibles of the newly rich and their wives in the narratives of David Graham Phillips. It was Phillips whose annoying talent for the exposure of abuses led Theodore Roosevelt to put the term "muck-raker" into currency.

While it is apparent that local-color stories, the historical novel, and the economic novel have all been borne in mind in choosing the titles for this important series of reprints, it is evident that careful consideration has also been given to treatments of various minority elements in the American population. The Negro, especially, but also the Indian, the half-breed, Creoles, Cajuns — and even the West Coast Japanese — appear as characters in various of these novels or volumes of short stories and sketches. Joel Chandler Harris's *Free Joe* will open the eyes of readers who know that author solely as the creator of humorous old Uncle Remus. And there is a revelatory volume of dialect tales, written by a Negro author, *The Conjure Woman* by Charles W. Chesnutt.

In literary conventions and the dominating attitudes toward life, the works in the Gregg series range from the adventurous romance illustrated so well by Mayne Reid or the polite urbanity of Owen Wister to the mordant irony of Kate Chopin and the grimmer realism of Joseph Kirkland's own experiences on bloody Civil War battlefields or the depressing display of New York farm life by Harold Frederic. In short, the series admirably illustrates the general qualities of the fiction produced in the United States during the era covered, just as it generously mirrors the geographical regions, the people, and the problems of the times.

CONTENTS.

The Great God Success.

I.

THE CANDIDATE FROM YALE.

"ON your college paper, I suppose?"

"No, I never wrote even a letter to the editor."

"Took prizes for essays?"

"No, I never wrote if I could help it."

"But you like to write?"

"I'd like to learn to write."

"You say you are two months out of college—what college?"

"Yale."

"Hum—I thought Yale men went into something commercial; law or banking or railroads. 'Leave hope of fortune behind, ye who enter here' is over the door of this profession."

"I haven't the money-making instinct."

"We pay fifteen dollars a week at the start."

"Couldn't you make it twenty?"

The Managing Editor of the *News-Record* turned slowly in his chair until his broad chest was full-front toward the young candidate for the staff. He lowered his florid face slowly until his double chin swelled out over his low "stick-up" collar. Then he gradually raised his eyelids until his amused blue eyes were looking over the tops of his glasses, straight into Howard's eyes.

"Why?" he asked. "Why should we?"

Howard's grey eyes showed embarrassment and he flushed to the line of his black hair which was so smoothly parted in the middle. "Well—you see—the fact is—I need twenty a week. My expenses are arranged on that scale. I'm not clever at money matters. I'm afraid I'd get in a mess with only fifteen."

"My dear young man," said Mr. King, "I started here at fifteen dollars a week. And I had a wife; and the first baby was coming."

"Yes, but your wife was an energetic woman. She stood right beside you and worked too. Now I have only myself."

Mr. King raised his eyebrows and became a rosier red. He was evidently preparing to rebuke this audacious intrusion into his private affairs by a stranger whose card had been handed to him not ten minutes before. But Howard's tone and manner were simple and sincere. And they happened to bring into Mr. King's mind a rush of memories of his youth and his wife. She had married him on faith. They had come to New York fifteen years before, he to get a place as reporter on the *News-Record*, she to start a boarding-house; he doubting and trembling, she with courage and confidence for two. He leaned back in his chair, closed his eyes and opened the book of memory at the place where the leaves most easily fell apart:

He is coming home at one in the morning, worn out, sick at heart from the day's buffetings. As he puts his key into the latch, the door opens. There stands a handsome girl; her face is flushed; her eyes are bright; her lips are held up for him to kiss; she shows no trace of a day that began hours before his and has been a succession of exasperations and humiliations against which her sensitive nature, trained in the home of her father, a distinguished up-the-state Judge, gives her no protection. "Victory," she whispers, her arms about his neck and her head upon his coat collar. "Victory! We are seventy-two cents ahead on the week, and everything paid up!"

Mr. King opened his eyes—they had been closed less than five seconds. "Well, let it be twenty—though just why I'm sure I don't know. And we'll give you a four weeks' trial. When will you begin?"

"Now," answered the young man, glancing about the room. "And I shall try to show that I appreciate your consideration, whether I deserve it or not."[1]

It was a large bare room, low of ceiling. Across one end were five windows overlooking from a great height the tempest that rages about the City Hall day and night with few lulls and no pauses. Mr. King's roll-top desk was at the first window. Under each of the other windows was a broad flat table desk —for copy-readers. At the farthest of these sat the City Editor—thin, precise-looking, with yellow skin, hollow cheeks, ragged grey-brown moustache, ragged scant grey-brown hair and dark brown eyes. He looked nervously tired and, because brown was his prevailing shade, dusty. He rose as Mr. King came with young Howard.

"Here, Mr. Bowring, is a young man from Yale. He wishes you to teach him how to write. Mr. Howard, Mr. Bowring. I hope you gentlemen will get on comfortably together."

Mr. King went back to his desk. Mr. Bowring and Howard looked each at the other. Mr. Bowring smiled, with good-humour, without cordiality. "Let me see, where shall we put you?" And his glance wandered along the rows of sloping table-desks—those nearer the windows lighted by daylight; those farther away, by electric lamps. Even on that cool, breezy August afternoon the sunlight and fresh air did not penetrate far into the room.

"Do you see the young man with the beautiful fair

moustache," said Mr. Bowring, "toiling away in his shirt-sleeves—there?"

"Near the railing at the entrance?"

"Precisely. I think I will put you next him." Mr. Bowring touched a button on his desk and presently an office boy—a mop of auburn curls, a pert face and gangling legs in knickerbockers—hurried up with a "Yes, Sir?"

"Please tell Mr. Kittredge that I would like to speak to him and—please scrape your feet along the floor as little as possible."

The boy smiled, walking away less as if he were trying to terrorize park pedestrians by a rush on roller skates. Kittredge and Howard were made acquainted and went toward their desks together. "A few moments—if you will excuse me—and I'm done," said Kittredge motioning Howard into the adjoining chair as he sat and at once bent over his work.

Howard watched him with interest, admiration and envy. The reporter was perhaps twenty-five years old—fair of hair, fair of skin, goodlooking in a pretty way. His expression was keen and experienced yet too self-complacent to be highly intelligent. He was rapidly covering sheet after sheet of soft white paper with bold, loose hand-writing. Howard noticed that at the end of each sentence he made a little cross with a circle about it, and that he began each paragraph with a paragraph sign. Presently he scrawled a big double cross in the centre of the sheet under the last line of writing and gathered up his sheets in the numbered order. "Done, thank God," he said. "And I hope they won't butcher it."

"Do you send it to be put in type?" asked Howard.

"No," Kittredge answered with a faint smile. "I hand it in to Mr. Bowring—the City Editor, you know. And when the copyreaders come at six, it will be turned over to one of them. He reads it, cuts it down if necessary, and writes headlines for it. Then it goes upstairs to the composing room—see the box, the little dumb-waiter, over there in the wall?—well, it goes up by that to the floor above where they set the type and make up the forms."

"I'm a complete ignoramus," said Howard, "I hope you'll not mind my trying to find out things. I hope I shall not bore you."

"Glad to help you, I'm sure. I had to go through this two years ago when I came here from Princeton."

Kittredge "turned in" his copy and returned to his seat beside Howard.

"What were you writing about, if I may ask?" inquired Howard.

"About some snakes that came this morning in a 'tramp' from South America. One of them, a boa constrictor, got loose and coiled around a windlass. The cook was passing and it caught him. He fainted with fright and the beast squeezed him to death. It's a fine story—lots of amusing and dramatic details. I wrote it for a column and I think they won't cut it. I hope not, anyhow. I need the money."

"You are paid by the column?"

"Yes. I'm on space—what they call a space writer. If a man is of any account here they gradually raise him to twenty-five dollars a week and then put him on space. That means that he will make anywhere from forty to a hundred a week, or perhaps more at times. The average for the best is about eighty."

"Eighty dollars a week," thought Howard. "Fifty-two times eighty is forty-one hundred and sixty. Four thousand a year, counting out two weeks for vacation." To Howard it seemed wealth at the limit of imagination. If he could make so much as that!—he who had grave doubts whether, no matter how hard he worked, he would ever wrench a living from the world.

Just then a seedy young man with red hair and a red beard came through the gate in the railing, nodded to Kittredge and went to a desk well up toward the daylight end of the room.

"That's the best of 'em all," said Kittredge in a low

tone. "His name is Sewell. He's a Harvard man—Harvard and Heidelberg. But drink! Ye gods, how he does drink! His wife died last Christmas—practically starvation. Sewell disappeared—frightful bust. A month afterward they found him under an assumed name over on Blackwell's Island, doing three months for disorderly conduct. He wrote a Christmas carol while his wife was dying. It began "Merrily over the Snow" and went on about light hearts and youth and joy and all that—you know, the usual thing. When he got the money, she didn't need it or anything else in her nice quiet grave over in Long Island City. So he 'blew in' the money on a wake."

Sewell was coming toward them. Kittredge called out: "Was it a good story, Sam?"

"Simply great! You ought to have seen the room. Only the bed and the cook-stove and a few dishes on a shelf—everything else gone to the pawnshop. The man must have killed the children first. They lay side by side on the bed, each with its hands folded on its chest—suppose the mother did that; and each little throat was cut from ear to ear—suppose the father did that. Then he dipped his paint brush in the blood and daubed on the wall in big scrawling letters: 'There is no God!' Then he took his wife in his arms, stabbed her to the heart and cut his own throat. And there they lay, his arms about her, his cheek against hers, dead. It was murder as a fine art. Gad, I wish I could write."

Kittredge introduced Howard—"a Yale man—just came on the paper."

"Entering the profession? Well, they say of the other professions that there is always room at the top. Journalism is just the reverse. The room is all at the bottom—easy to enter, hard to achieve, impossible to leave. It is all bottom, no top." Sewell nodded, smiled attractively in spite of his swollen face and his unsightly teeth, and went back to his work.

"He's sober," said Kittredge when he was out of hearing, "so his story is pretty sure to be the talk of Park Row to-morrow."

Howard was astonished at the cheerful, businesslike point of view of these two educated and apparently civilised young men as to the tragedies of life. He had shuddered at Kittredge's story of the man squeezed to death by the snake. Sewell's story, so graphically outlined, filled him with horror, made it a struggle for him to conceal his feelings.

"I suppose you must see a lot of frightful things," he suggested.

"That's our business. You soon get used to it, just as a doctor does. You learn to look at life from the purely professional standpoint. Of course you must feel in order to write. But you must not feel so keenly that you can't write. You have to remember always that you're not there to cheer or sympathise or have emotions, but only to report, to record. You tell what your eyes see. You'll soon get so that you can and will make good stories out of your own calamaties."

"Is that a portrait of the editor?" asked Howard, pointing to a grimed oil-painting, the only relief to the stretch of cracked and streaked white wall except a few ragged maps.

"That—oh, that is old man Stone—the 'great condenser.' He's there for a double purpose, as an example of what a journalist should be and as a warning of what a journalist comes to. After twenty years of fine work at crowding more news in good English into one column than any other editor could get in bad English into four columns, he was discharged for drunkenness. Soon afterwards he walked off the end of a dock one night in a fog. At least it was said that there was a fog and that he was drunk. I have my doubts."

"Cheerful! I have not been in the profession an hour but I have already learned something very valuable."

"What's that?" asked Kittredge, "that it's a good profession to get out of?"

"No. But that bad habits will not help a man to a

career in journalism any more than in any other profession."

"Career?" smiled Kittredge, resenting Howard's good-humoured irony and putting on a supercilious look that brought out more strongly the insignificance of his face. "Journalism is not a career. It is either a school or a cemetery. A man may use it as a stepping-stone to something else. But if he sticks to it, he finds himself an old man, dead and done for to all intents and purposes years before he's buried."

"I wonder if it doesn't attract a great many men who have a little talent and fancy that they have much. I wonder if it does not disappoint their vanity rather than their merit."

"That sounds well," replied Kittredge, "and there's some truth in it. But, believe me, journalism is the dragon that demands the annual sacrifice of youth. It will have only youth. Why am I here? Why are you here? Because we are young, have a fresh, a new point of view. As soon as we get a little older, we shall be stale and, though still young in years, we must step aside for young fellows with new ideas and a new point of view."

"But why should not one have always new ideas, always a new point of view? Why should one expect to escape the penalties of stagnation in journalism when one can't escape them in any other profession?"

"But who has new ideas all the time? The average successful man has at most one idea and makes a whole career out of it. Then there are the temptations."

"How do you mean?"

Kittredge flushed slightly and answered in a more serious tone:

"We must work while others amuse themselves or sleep. We must sleep while others are at work. That throws us out of touch with the whole world of respectability and regularity. When we get done at night, wrought up by the afternoon and evening of this gambling with our brains and nerves as the stake, what is open to us?"

"That is true," said Howard. "There are the all-night saloons and—the like."

"And if we wish society, what society is open to us? What sort of young women are waiting to entertain us at one, two, three o'clock in the morning? Why, I have not made a call in a year. And I have not seen a respectable girl of my acquaintance in at least that time, except once or twice when I happened to have assignments that took me near Fifth Avenue in the afternoon."

"Mr. Kittredge, Mr. Bowring wishes to speak to you," an office boy said and Kittredge rose. As he went, he put his hand on Howard's shoulder and said:

"No, I am getting out of it as fast as ever I can. I'm writing books."

"Kittredge," thought Howard, "I wonder, is this Henry Jennings Kittredge, whose stories are on all the news stands?" He saw an envelope on the floor at his feet. The address was "Henry Jennings Kittredge, Esq."

When Kittredge came back for his coat, Howard said in a tone of frank admiration: "Why, I didn't know you were the Kittredge that everybody is talking about. *You* certainly have no cause for complaint."

Kittredge shrugged his shoulders. "At fifteen cents a copy, I have to sell ten thousand copies before I get enough to live on for four months. And you'd be surprised how much reputation and how little money a man can make out of a book. Don't be distressed because they keep you here with nothing to do but wonder how you'll have the courage to face the cashier on pay day. It's the system. Your chance will come."

It was three days before Howard had a chance. On a Sunday afternoon the Assistant City Editor who was in charge of the City Desk for the day sent him up to the Park to write a descriptive story of the crowds. "Try to get a new point of view," he said, "and let yourself loose. There's usually plenty of room in Monday's paper."

Howard wandered through the Central Park for two hours, struggling for the "new point of view" of the crowds he saw there—these monotonous millions, he thought, lazily drinking at a vast trough of country air in the heart of the city. He planned an article carefully as he dined alone at the Casino. He went down to the office early and wrote diligently—about two thousand words. When he had finished, the Night City Editor told him that he might go as there would be nothing more that night.

He was in the street at seven the next morning. As he walked along with a *News-Record*, bought at the first news-stand, he searched every page: first, the larger "heads"—such a long story would call for a "big head;" then the smaller "heads"—they may have been crowded and have had to cut it down; then the single-line "heads"—surely they found a "stickful" or so worth printing.

At last he found it. A dozen items in the smallest type, agate, were grouped under the general heading "City Jottings" at the end of an inside column of an inside page. The first of these City Jottings was two lines in length:

"The millions were in the Central Park yesterday, lazily drinking at that vast trough of country air in the heart of the city."

As he entered the office Howard looked appealingly and apologetically at the boy on guard at the railing and braced himself to receive the sneering frown of the City Editor and to bear the covert smiles of his fellow reporters. But he soon saw that no one had observed his mighty spring for a foothold and his ludicrous miss and fall.

"Had anything in yet?" Kittredge inquired casually, late in the afternoon.

"I wrote a column and a half yesterday and I found two lines among the City Jottings," replied Howard, reddening but laughing.

"The first story I wrote was cut to three lines but they got a libel suit on it."

II.

THE CITY EDITOR RECONSIDERS.

At the end of six weeks, the City Editor called Howard up to the desk and asked him to seat himself. He talked in a low tone so that the Assistant City Editor, reading the newspapers at a near-by desk, could not hear.

"We like you, Mr. Howard." Mr. Bowring spoke slowly and with a carefulness in selecting words that indicated embarrassment. "And we have been impressed by your earnestness. But we greatly fear that you are not fitted for this profession. You write well enough, but you do not seem to get the newspaper—the news—idea. So we feel that in justice to you and to ourselves we ought to let you know where you stand. If you wish, we shall be glad to have you remain with us two weeks longer. Meanwhile you can be looking about you. I am certain that you will succeed somewhere, in some line, sooner or later. But I think that the newspaper profession is a waste of your time."

Howard had expected this. Failure after failure, his articles thrown away or re-written by the copyreaders, had prepared him for the blow. Yet it crushed him for the moment. His voice was not steady as he replied :

" No doubt you are right. Thank you for taking the trouble to study my case and tell me so soon."

" Don't hesitate to stay on for the two weeks," Mr. Bowring continued. " We can make you useful to us. And you can look about to much better advantage than if you were out of a place."

" I'll stay the two weeks," Howard said, " unless I find something sooner."

" Don't be more discouraged than you can help," said Mr. Bowring. " You may be very grateful before long for finding out so early what many of us—I myself, I fear—find out after years and—when it is too late."

Always that note of despair; always that pointing to the motto over the door of the profession : " Abandon hope, ye who enter here." What was the explanation? Were these men right? Was he wrong in thinking that journalism offered the most splendid of careers—the development of the mind and the character : the sharpening of all the faculties ; the service of truth and right and human betterment, in daily combat with injustice and error and falsehood ; the arousing and stimulating of the drowsy minds of the masses of mankind?

Howard looked about at the men who held on where he was slipping. "Can it be," he thought, "that I cannot survive in a profession where the poorest are so poor in intellect and equipment? Why am I so dull that I cannot catch the trick?"

He set himself to study newspapers, reading them line by line, noting the modes of presenting facts, the arrangement of headlines, the order in which the editors put the several hundred items before the eyes of the reader—what they displayed on each page and why; how they apportioned the space. With the energy of unconquerable resolution he applied himself to solving for himself the puzzle of the press—the science and art of catching the eye and holding the attention of the hurrying, impatient public.

He learned much. He began to develop the news-instinct, that subtle instant realisation of what is interesting and what is not interesting to the public mind. But the time was short; a sense of impending calamity and the lack of self-confidence natural to inexperience made it impossible for him effectively to use his new knowledge in the few small opportunities which Mr. Bowring gave him. With only six days of his two weeks left, he had succeeded in getting into the paper not a single item of a length greater than two sticks. He slept little; he despaired not at all; but he was heart-sick and, as he lay in his bed in the little hall-room of the furnished-room house, he often envied women the relief of tears. What he endured will be appreciated only by those who have been bred in sheltered homes; who have abruptly and alone struck out for themselves in the ocean of a great city without a single lesson in swimming; who have felt themselves seized from below and dragged downward toward the deep-lying feeding-grounds of Poverty and Failure.

"Buck up, old man," said Kittredge to whom he told his bad news after several days of hesitation and after Kittredge had shown him that he strongly suspected it. "Don't mind old Bowring. You're sure to get on, and, if you insist upon the folly, in this profession. I'll give you a note to Montgomery—he's City Editor over at the *World*-shop—and he'll take you on. In some ways you will do better there. You'll rise faster, get a wider experience, make more money. In fact, this shop has only one advantage. It does give a man peace of mind. It's more like a club than an office. But in a sense that is a drawback. I'll give you a note to-night. You will be at work over there to-morrow."

"I think I'll wait a few days," said Howard, his tone corresponding to the look in his eyes and the compression of his resolute mouth.

The next day but one Mr. Bowring called him up

to the City Desk and gave him a newspaper-clipping which read:

"Bald Peak, September 29—Willie Dent, the three-year-old baby of John Dent, a farmer living two miles from here, strayed away into the mountains yesterday and has not been seen since. His dog, a cur, went with him. Several hundred men are out searching. It has been storming, and the mountains are full of bears and wild cats."

"Yes, I saw this in the *Herald*," said Howard.

"Will you take the train that leaves at eleven to-night and get us the story—if it is not a 'fake,' as I strongly suspect. Telegraph your story if there is not time for you to get back here by nine to-morrow night."

"Of course it's a fake, or at least a wild exaggeration," thought Howard as he turned away. "If Bowring had not been all but sure there was nothing in it, he would never have given it to me."

He was not well, his sleepless nights having begun to tell even upon his powerful constitution. The rest of that afternoon and all of a night without sleep in the Pullman he was in a depth of despond. He had been in the habit of getting much comfort out of an observation his father had made to him just before he died: "Remember that ninety per cent of these fourteen hundred million human beings are uncertain where to-morrow's food is to come from. Be prudent but never be afraid." But just then he could get no consolation out of this maxim of grim cheer. He seemed to himself incompetent and useless, a predestined failure. "What is to become of me?" he kept repeating, his heart like lead and his mind fumbling about in a confused darkness.

At Bald Peak he was somewhat revived by the cold mountain air of the early morning. As he alighted upon the station platform he spoke to the baggage-master standing in front of the steps.

"Was the little boy of a man named Dent lost in the mountains near here?"

"Yes—three days ago," replied the baggage-man.

"Have they found him yet?"

"No—nor never will alive—that's my opinion."

Howard asked for the nearest livery-stable and within twenty minutes was on his way to Dent's farm. His driver knew all about the lost child. Two hundred men were still searching. "And Mrs. Dent, she's been sittin' by the window, list'nin' day and night. She won't speak nor eat and she ain't shed a tear. It was her only child. The men come in sayin' it ain't no use to hunt any more, an' they look at her an' out they goes ag'in."

Soon the driver pointed to a cottage near the road. The gate was open; the grass and the flower-beds were trampled into a morass. The door was thrown wide and several women were standing about the threshold. At the window within view of the road and the mountains sat the mother—a young woman with large brown eyes, and clear-cut features, refined, beautified, exalted by suffering. Her look was that of one listening for a faint, far away sound upon which hangs the turn of the balances to joy or to despair.

* * * * * * * * *

That morning two of the searchers went to the northeast into the dense and tangled swamp woods between Bald Peak and Cloudy Peak—the wildest wilderness in the mountains. The light barely penetrates the foliage on the brightest days. The ground is rough, sometimes precipitous, closely covered with bushes and tangled creepers.

The two explorers, almost lost themselves, came at last to the edge of a swamp surrounded by cedars. They half-crawled, half-climbed through the low trees and festooning creepers to the edge of a clear bit of open, firm ground.

In the middle was a cedar tree. Under it, seated upon the ground, was the lost boy. His bare, brown legs, torn and bleeding, were stretched straight in front of him. His bare feet were bruised and cut. His gingham dress was torn and wet and stained. His small hands were smears of dirt and blood. He was playing with a tin can. He had put a stone into it and was making a great rattling. The dog was running to and fro, apparently enjoying the noise. The little boy's face was tear-stained and his eyes were swollen. But he was not crying just then and laughter lurked in his thin, fever-flushed face.

As the men came into view, the dog began to bark angrily, but the boy looked a solemn welcome.

"Want mamma," he said. "I'se hungry."

One of the men picked him up—the gingham dress was saturated.

"You're hungry?" asked the man, his voice choking.

"Yes. An' I'se so wet. It wained and wained." Then the child began to sob. "It was dark," he whispered, "an' cold. I want my mamma."

It was an hour's tedious journey back to Dent's by the shortest route. At the top of the hill those near the cottage saw the boy in the arms of the man who had found him. They shouted and the mother sprang out of the house and came running, stumbling down the path to the gate. She caught at the gate-post and stood there, laughing, screaming, sobbing.

"Baby! Baby!" she called.

The little boy turned his head and stretched out his thin, blood-stained arms. She ran toward him and snatched him from the young farmer.

"Hungry, mamma," he sobbed, hiding his face on her shoulder.

* * * * * * * * *

Howard wrote his story on the train, going down to New York. It was a straightforward chronicle of just what he had seen and heard. He began at the beginning—the little mountain home, the family of three, the disappearance of the child. He described the perils of the mountains, the storm, the search, the wait, the listening mother, scene by scene, ending with mother and child together again and the dog racing around them, with wagging tail and hanging tongue. He wrote swiftly, making no changes, without a trace of his usual self-consciousness in composition. When he had done he went into the restaurant car and dined almost gaily. He felt that he had failed again. How could he hope to tell such a story? But he was not despondent. He was still under the spell of that intense human drama with its climax of joy. His own concerns seemed secondary, of no consequence.

He reached the office at half-past nine, handed in his "copy" and went away. He was in bed at half-past ten and was at once asleep. At eleven the next morning a knocking awakened him from a sound sleep that had restored and refreshed him. "A messenger from the office," was called through the door in answer to his inquiry. He took the note from the boy and tore it open:

"My dear Mr. Howard: Thank you for the splendid story you gave us last night. It is one of the best, if not the best, we have had the pleasure of publishing in years. Your salary has been raised to twenty-five dollars a week.

"Congratulations. You have 'caught on' at last. I'm glad to take back what I said the other day.

"HENRY C. BOWRING."

III.

A PARK ROW CELEBRITY.

KITTREDGE was the first to congratulate him when he reached the office. " Everybody is talking about your story," he said. " I must say I was surprised when I read it. I had begun to fear that you would never catch the trick—for, with most of us writing is only a trick. But now I see that you are a born writer. Your future is in your own hands."

" You think I can learn to write ? "

" That is the sane way to put it. Yes, I know that you can. If you'll only not be satisfied with the results that come easy, you will make a reputation. Not a mere Park Row reputation, but the real thing."

Howard got flattery enough in the next few days to turn a stronger head than was his at twenty-two. But a few partial failures within a fortnight sobered him and steadied him. His natural good sense made him take himself in hand. He saw that his success had been to a great extent a happy accident ; that to repeat it, to improve upon it he must study life, study the art of expression. He must keep his senses open to impression. He must work at style, enlarge his vocabulary, learn the use of words, the effect of varying combinations of words both as to sound and as to meaning. "I must learn to write for the people," he thought, "and that means to write the most difficult of all styles."

He was, then and always, one of those who like others and are liked by them, yet never seek company and so are left to themselves. As he had no money to spare and a deep aversion to debt, he was not tempted into joining in the time-wasting dissipations that were now open to him. He worked hard at his profession and, when he left the office, usually went direct to his rooms to read until far into the morning. He was often busy sixteen hours out of the twenty-four. His day at reporting was long—from noon until midnight, and frequently until three in the morning. But the work was far different from the grind which is the lot of the young men striving in other professions or in business. It was the most fascinating work imaginable for an intelligent, thirsty mind—the study of human nature under stress of the great emotions.

His mode of thought and his style made Mr. Bowring and Mr. King give him much of this particular kind of reporting. So he was always observing love, hate, jealousy, revenge, greed. He saw these passions in action in the lives of people of all kinds and conditions. And he saw little else. The reporter is a historian. And history is, as Gibbon says, for the most part "a record of the crimes, follies and misfortunes of mankind."

For many a man this has been a ruinous, one-sided development. Howard was saved by his extremely intelligent, sympathetic point of view. He saw the whole of each character, each conflict that he was sent to study. If the point of the story was the good side of human nature—some act of generosity or self-sacrifice—he did not exaggerate it into godlike heroism but adjusted it in its proper prospective by bringing out its human quality and its human surroundings. If the main point was violence or sordidness or baseness, he saw the characteristics which relieved and partially redeemed it. His news-reports were accounts of the doings not of angels or devils but of human beings, accounts written from a thoroughly human standpoint.

Here lay the cause of his success. In all his better stories—for he often wrote poor ones—there was the atmosphere of sincerity, of realism, the marks of an acute observer, without prejudice and with a justifiable leaning toward a belief in the fundamental worth of humanity. Where others were cynical he was just. Where others were sentimental, he had sincere, healthful sentiment. Where others were hysterical, he calmly and accurately described, permitting the tragedy to reveal itself instead of burying it beneath high-heaped adjectives. Simplicity of style was his aim and he was never more delighted by any compliment than by one from the chief political reporter.

"That story of yours this morning," said this reporter whose lack as a writer was more than compensated by his ability to get intimately acquainted with public men, "reads as if a child might have written it. I don't see how you get such effects without any style at all. You just let your story tell itself."

"Well, you see," replied Howard, "I am writing for the masses, and fine writing would be wasted upon them."

"You're right," said Jackman, "we don't need literature on this paper—long words, high-sounding phrases and all that sort of thing. What we want is just plain, simple English that goes straight to the point."

"Like Shakespeare's and Bunyan's," suggested Kittredge with a grin.

"Shakespeare? Fudge!" scoffed Jackman. "Why he couldn't have made a living as a space-writer on a New York newspaper."

"No, I don't think he would have staid long in Park Row," replied Kittredge with a subtlety of meaning that escaped Jackman.

* * * * * * * * *

A few days before New Year's the Managing Editor looked up and smiled as Howard was passing his desk. "How goes it?" he asked.

"Oh, not so badly," Howard answered, "but I am a good deal depressed at times."

"Depressed? Nonsense! You've got everything —youth, health and freedom. And by the way, you are going on space the first of the year. Our rule is a year on salary before space. But we felt that it was about time to strengthen the rule by making an exception.'

Howard stammered thanks and went away. This piece of news, dropped apparently so carelessly by Mr. King, meant a revolution in fortune for him. It was the transition from close calculation on twenty-five dollars a week to wealth beyond his most fanciful dreams of six months ago. Not having the money-getting instinct and being one of those who compare their work with the best instead of with the inferior, Howard never felt that he was "entitled to a living." He had a lively sense of gratitude for the money return for his services which prudence presently taught him to conceal.

"Space" meant to him eighty dollars a week at least—circumstances of ease. So vast a sum did it seem that he began to consider the problem of investment. "I have been not badly off on twenty-five dollars a week," he thought. "With, well, say forty dollars a week I shall be able to satisfy all my wants. I can save at least forty a week and that will mean an independence with a small income by the time I am thirty-four."

But—a year after he was put "on space" he was still just about even with his debts. He seemed to himself to be living no better and it was only by careful counting-up that he could see how that dream of independence had eluded him. A more extensive wardrobe, a little better food, a more comfortable suite of rooms, an occasional dinner to some friends, loans to broken-down reporters, and the mysteriously vanished two thousand dollars was accounted for.

Howard tried to retrench, devised small ingenious schemes for saving money, lectured himself severely and frequently for thus trifling away his chance to be a free man. But all in vain. He remained poor; and, whenever he gave the matter thought, which was not often, gloomy forebodings as to the future oppressed him. "I shall find myself old," he thought, "with nothing accomplished, with nothing laid by. I shall be an old drudge." He understood the pessimistic tone of his profession. All about him were men like himself—leading this gambler's life of feverish excitement and evanescent achievement, earning comfortable incomes and saving nothing, looking forward to the inevitable time of failing freshness and shattered nerves and declining income.

He spasmodically tried to write stories for the magazines, contrived plots for novels and plays, wrote first chapters, first scenes of first acts. But the exactions of newspaper life, the impossibility of continuous effort at any one piece of work and his natural inertia—he was inert but neither idle nor lazy—combined to make futile his efforts to emancipate himself from hand-to-mouth journalism.

He had been four years a reporter and was almost twenty-six years old. He was known throughout his profession in New York, although he had never signed an article. One remarkable "human interest" story after another had forced the knowledge of his abilities upon the reporters and editors of other newspapers. And he was spoken of as one of the best and in some respects the best "all round reporter" in the city. This meant that he was capable to any emergency—that, whatever the subject, he could write an accurate, graphic, consecutive and sustained story and could get it into the editor's hands quickly.

Indeed he possessed facility to the perilous degree. What others achieved only after long toil, he achieved without effort. This was due chiefly to the fact that he never relaxed but was at all times the journalist, reading voraciously newspapers, magazines and the best books, and using what he read; observing constantly and ever trying to see something that would make "good copy"; turning over phrases in his mind to test the value of words both as to sound and as to meaning. He was an incessantly active man. His great weakness was the common weakness—failure to concentrate. In Park Row they regarded him as a brilliant success. Brilliant he was. But a success he was not. He knew that he was a brilliant failure—and not very brilliant.

"Why is it?" he asked himself again and again in periods of reaction from the nervous strain of some exciting experience. "Shall I never seize any of these chances that are always thrusting themselves at me? Shall I always act like a Neapolitan beggar? Will the stimulus to ambition never come?"

IV.

IN THE EDGE OF BOHEMIA.

HOWARD lived in Washington Square, South. He had gone to a "furnished-room house" there because it was cheap. He staid because he was comfortable and was without a motive for moving.

It was the centre of the most varied life in New York. To the north lay fashion and wealth, to the east and west, respectability and moderate means; to the south, poverty and squalor, vice and crime. All could be seen and heard from the windows of his sitting room. In the evenings toward spring he looked out upon a panorama of the human race such as is presented by no other city in the world and by no other part of that city. Within view were Americans of all kinds, French and Germans, Italians and Austrians, Spaniards and Moors, Scandinavians and negroes, born New Yorkers and born citizens of most of the capitals of civilisation and semi-barbarism. There were actresses, dancers, shop girls, cocottes; touts, thieves, confidence-men, mission workers; artists and students from the musty University building, tramps and drunkards from the "barrel-houses" and "stale-beer shops;" and, across the square to the north, representatives of New York's oldest and most noted families. To the west were apartment houses whence stiff, prim bookkeepers, floor-walkers, clerks and small shop-keepers issued with their families on Sundays, bound for church. There were other apartment houses—the most of them to the south—whence in the midnight hours came slattern servants and reckless looking girls in loose wrappers and high-heeled slippers, pitcher in hand, bound for the nearest saloon.

After dusk from early spring until late fall a multitude of interesting sounds mingled with the roar of the elevated trains to the west and south and the rumble of carriages in "the Avenue" to the north. Howard, reading or writing at his window on his leisure days, heard the young men and young women laughing and shouting and making love under the trees where the Washington Arch glistened in the twilight. Later came the songs—"I want you, my honey, yes I do," or "Lu, Lu, how I love my Lu!", or some other of the current concert-hall jingles. Many figures could be seen flitting about in the shadows. Usually these figures were in pairs; usually one was in white; usually at her waist-line there was a black belt that continued on until it was lost in the other and darker figure.

Scraps of a score of languages—curses, jests, terms

of endearment—would float up to him. Then came the hours of comparative silence, with the city breathing softly and regularly, with the moon hanging low and the pale arch rising above the dark trees like a giant ghost. There would be an occasional drunken shout or shriek; a riotous roar of song from some staggering reveller making company for himself on the journey home; the heavy step of the policeman. Or perhaps the only sound to disturb the city's sleep would be that soft tread, timid as a mouse's, stealthy as a jackal's—the tread of a lonely woman with draggled silk skirt and painted cheeks and eyes burning into the darkness, and a heart as bitter and as sad as no money, no home, no friends, no hope can make it.

Once he threw a silver dollar from his window to the sidewalk well in front of her. She did not see it flash downward but she heard it ring upon the walk. She rushed forward and twice kicked it away from her in her frenzy to get it. When her bare hand—or was it a claw?—at last closed upon it, she gave a low scream, looked slyly and fearfully about, then ran as if death were at her heels.

Soon after Howard was put "on space" he took the best suite of rooms in the house. It was a strange company which Mrs. Sands had gathered under her roof. Except Howard there was no one, not even Mrs. Sands herself, who did not have so much past that there was little left for future. Indeed, perhaps none of these storm-tossed or wrecked human craft had had more of a past than Mrs. Sands. There was no mistaking the significance of those deep furrows filled with powder and plastered with paint, those few hairs tinted and frizzed. But like all persons with real pasts Mrs. Sands and her lodgers kept the veil tightly drawn. They confessed to no yesterdays and they did not dare think of to-morrow. They were incuriously awaiting the impulse which was sure to come, sure to thrust them on downward.

A new lodger at Mrs. Sand's usually took the best rooms that were to be had. Then, sometimes slowly, sometimes swiftly, came the retreat upward until a cubby-hole under the eaves was reached. Finally came precipitate and baggageless departure, often with a week or two of lodging unpaid. The next pause, if pause there was, would be still nearer the river-bed or the Morgue.

One morning when he had been living in Washington Square, South, about three years, Howard was dressing hurriedly, the door of his sitting-room accidentally ajar. Through the crack he saw some one stooping over the serving tray which he had himself put outside his door when he had finished breakfast. He looked more closely. It was "the clergyman" from up under the eaves—an unfrocked priest, thin to emaciation, misery written upon his face even more deeply than weakness. He hastily bundled the bones of two chops and a bit of bread into a stained and torn handkerchief, and sprang away up the stairs toward his little hole at the roof.

Howard was in a hurry and so put off for the time action upon the natural impulse. When he came back at midnight, there was soon a knock at his door. He opened it and invited in the man at the threshold —a tall, strongly built, erect German, with a dissipated handsome face, heavily scarred from university duels.

"Pardon me for disturbing you," said the German. His speech, his tone, his manner, left no doubt as to his breeding though they raised the gravest doubts as to his being willing to give a true account of why he had become a tenant in that lodging house.

"Will you have a cigarette and some whiskey?" inquired Howard.

The German's glance lit and lingered upon the bottle of Scotch on the table. "Concentrated, double-distilled friendship," said he as he poured out his drink.

"But a friend that drives all others away," smiled Howard.

"I have found it of a very jealous disposition," replied the German with a careless shrug of the shoulders and a lifting of the eyebrows. "But at least this friend has the grace to stay after it has driven the others away."

"To stay until the last piece of silver is gone."

"But what more does one expect of a friend? Besides, we are overlooking one friend—the one who helped our clerical fellow-lodger of the attic out of his troubles to-day."

"His luck has turned?"

"Permanently. He shot himself this afternoon."

"And only this morning I made up my mind to try to help him," said Howard regretfully.

"You could not have hoped to succeed so well. His case needed something more than temporary expedient. But, to come to the point, I had a slight acquaintance with him. He left a note for me—mailed it just before he shot himself. In it he asked that I insert a personal in the *Herald*. Unfortunately I have not the money. I thought that you as a journalist might be able to suggest something."

The German held out a slip of cheap writing paper on which was written: "Helen—when you see this it will be over—L."

"A good story," was Howard's first thought, his news-instinct alert. And then he remembered that it was not for him to tell. "I will attend to this for you to-morrow."

"Thank you," said the German, helping himself to the whiskey. "Have you seen the new lodgers?"

"Those in the room behind me? Yes. I saw them at the front door as I came in."

"They're a queer pair—the youngest I've seen in this house. I've been wondering what tempest wrecked them on this forlorn coast so early in the voyage."

"Why wrecked?"

"My dear sir, we are all—except you—wrecks here, all unseaworthy at least."

"One of them was quite pretty, I thought," said Howard, "the slender one with the black hair."

"They are not mates. The other girl is of a different sort. She's more used to this kind of life, at least to poverty. I fancy Miss Black-Hair looks on it as a lark. But she'll find out the truth by the time she has mounted another story."

"Here, to go up means to go down," Howard said, weary of the conversation and wishing that the German would leave.

"They say that they're sisters," the German went on, again helping himself to the whiskey; "They say they have run away from home because of a step-mother and that they are going to earn their own living. But they won't. They spend the nights racing about with a gang of the young wretches of this neighbourhood. They won't be able to stand getting up early for work. And then——"

The German blew out a huge cloud of cigarette smoke, shrugged his shoulders and added: "Miss Black-Hair may get on up town presently. But I doubt it. The Tenderloin rarely recruits from down here."

The bottle was empty and the German bowed himself out. As the night was hot, Howard opened the door a few moments afterward. At the other end of the short hall light was streaming through the open door of the room the two girls had taken. Before he could turn, there was a shadow and "Miss Black-Hair" was standing in her doorway.

"Oh," she began, "I thought——"

Howard paused, looking at her. She was above the medium height—tall for a woman—and slender. Her loose wrapper, a little open at her round throat, clung to her, attracting attention to all the lines of her form. Her hair was indeed black, jet black, waving back from her forehead in a line of curving and beautiful irregularity. Her skin was clear and dark. There were deep circles under her eyes, making them look unnaturally large, pathetically weary. In repose her face was childish and sadly serious. When she smiled she looked older and pert, but no happier.

"I thought," she continued with the pert, self-confident smile, "that you were my sister Nellie. I'm waiting for her."

"You're in early to-night," said Howard, the circles under her eyes reminding him of what the German had told him.

"I haven't slept much for a week," the girl replied, "I'm nearly dead. But I won't go to bed till Nellie comes."

Howard was about to turn when she went on: "We agreed always to stay together. She broke it to-night. My fellow got too fresh, so I came home. She said she'd come too. That was an hour ago and she isn't here yet."

"Isn't she rather young to be out alone at this time?"

Howard could hardly have told why he continued the conversation. He certainly would not, had she been less beautiful or less lonely and childish. At his remark about her sister's youth she laughed with an expression of cunning at once amusing and pitiful.

"She's a year older than me," she said, "and I guess I can take care of myself. Still she hasn't much sense. She'll get into trouble yet. She doesn't understand how to manage the boys when they're too fresh."

"But you do, I suppose?" suggested Howard.

"Indeed I do," with a quick nod of her small

graceful head, "I know what I'm about. *My* mother taught *me* a few things."

"Didn't she teach your sister also?"

"Miss Black-Hair" dropped her eyes and flushed a little, looking like a child caught in a lie. "Of course," she said after a pause.

"How long have you been without your mother?"

"I've been away from home four months. But I saw her in the street yesterday. She didn't see me though."

"Then you've got a step-father?"

"No, I haven't. Nellie told that to Mrs. Sands. But it's not so. You know Nellie's not my sister?"

"I fancied not from what you said a moment ago."

"No, she used to be nurse girl in our family. We just say we're sisters. I wish she'd come. I'm tired of standing. Won't you come in?"

She went into her room, her manner a frank and simple invitation. Howard hesitated, then went just inside the door and half sat, half leaned upon the high roll of the lounge. The room was cheaply furnished, the lounge and a closed folding bed almost filling it. Upon the mantel, the bureau and the little table were a few odds and ends that stamped it a woman's room. A street gown of thin pale-blue cloth was thrown over a rocking chair. As the girl leaned back in this chair with her face framed in the pale-blue of the gown, she looked tired and sad and beautiful and very young.

"If Nellie doesn't look out, I'll go away and live alone," she said, and the accompanying unconscious look of loneliness touched Howard.

"You might go back home."

"You don't know my home or you wouldn't say that. You don't know my father." She had got upon the subject of herself, and, once in that road she kept it with no thought of turning out. "He can't treat me as he treats mother. Why, he goes away and stays for days. Then he comes home and quarrels with her all the time. They never both sit through a meal. One or the other flares up and leaves. He generally whipped me when he got very mad—just for spite."

"But there's your mother."

"Yes. She doesn't like my going away. But I can't stand it. Papa wouldn't let me go anywhere or let anybody come to see me. He says everybody's bad. I guess he's about right. Only he doesn't include himself."

"You seem to have a poor opinion of people."

"Well, you can't blame me." She put on her wise look of experience and craft. "I've been away, living with Nellie for four months and I've seen no good to speak of. A girl doesn't get a fair chance."

"But you've got work?"

"Oh, yes. We both stayed down in a restaurant.

Nellie's got a place as waiter. That's the best she could do. The man said I was good-looking and would catch trade. So he made me cashier. I get six dollars a week to Nellie's three. But it's a bad place. The men are always slipping notes in my hand when they give me their checks. Then the boss, he's always bothering around."

"But you don't have to work hard?"

"From nine till four. We get our lunch free. I pay three dollars on the room and Nellie pays one."

If Howard had not seen many such problems in economics before, he would have been astonished at any one even hoping to be able to get two meals a day, clothing and carfare out of two or three dollars a week. As it was, he only wondered how long a girl who had been used at least to comfort would endure this. "It's easy for the other girl," he thought, "because she's used to it. But this one—" and he decided that the "trouble" would begin as soon as her clothing was worn out.

He noticed that she was pulling at the third finger of her right hand where she would have worn rings if she had had any. "You've had to pawn your rings?" he ventured.

She looked at him startled. "Did Nellie tell you?" she asked.

"No," he replied, "I saw that you were missing your rings and suspected the rest."

"Yes; that's so. I've pawned all my jewelry except a bracelet. Nellie can't get along on her three dollars. She eats too much."

"I should think you'd rather be at home."

"As I told you before," she said impatiently, "anything's better than home. Besides, I'm pretty well off. I go where I please, stay out as late as I please and have all the company I want. At home I'd have to be in bed at ten o'clock."

There was a sound at the front door down in the darkness. The girl started from the chair, listened, then exclaimed: "There she comes now. And it's two o'clock!"

Howard took the hint, smiled and said: "Well, good-night. I'll see you again."

"Good-night," the girl answered absently.

From his room Howard heard Nellie coming up the stairs. "You're a nice one!" came in "Miss Black-Hair's" indignant voice, "Where have you been? Where did you and Jack go?"

The answer came in a sob—"Oh, Alice, you'll never forgive me!"

Their door closed upon the two girls but Howard could still hear Nellie's voice tearful, pleading. There was the sound of some one falling heavily upon the lounge, then sobs and cries of "Oh! Oh!" As Howard went into his bedroom, he could hear the voices still more plainly through the thin wall. He caught the words only once. "Miss Black-Hair," her voice shaking with anger, exclaimed: "Nellie Baker, you are a wicked girl, I shall go away."

V.

ALICE.

SEVERAL nights later Howard came upon Alice at the front door, where a young man was detaining her in a lingering good-bye. Another night as he was passing her room he saw her stretched upon the floor, her head supported by her elbows and an open book in front of her. She looked so childlike that Howard paused and said: "What is it—a fairy story?"

"No, it's a love story," she replied, just glancing at him with a faint smile and showing that she did not wish to be interrupted. The same night as he was going to bed he heard the angry voices of the two girls. A week later, toward the end of July, he found Alice sitting on the front stoop, when he came from dinner. She was obviously in the depths of the "blues." Her eyes, the droop of the corners of her mouth, even the colour of her skin indicated anxiety and depression. She looked so forlorn that he said gently: "Wouldn't you like to walk in the Square?"

She rose at once. "Yes, I guess so." They crossed to the green. She was wearing the pale-blue gown and it fitted her well. Neither in the gown nor in the big hat with its coquettish flowers nodding over the brim was there much of fashion. But there was a certain distinction in her walk and her manner of wearing her clothes; and to a pretty face and a graceful form was added the charm of youth, magnetic youth.

"Do you want to walk?" she asked, lassitude in her voice.

"No, let us sit," he said, and they went to a bench near the arch. It was twilight. The children were still romping and shouting. Many fat elderly women—mothers and grandmothers—were solemnly marching about, talking in fat, elderly voices.

"You have the blues?" asked Howard, thinking it might make her feel better to talk of her troubles. "If I were your doctor, I should prescribe a series of good cries."

"I don't cry," said the girl. "Sometimes I wish I could. Nellie cries and gets over things. I feel awful inside and sick and my eyes burn. But I can't cry."

"You're too young for that."

"Oh, in some ways I'm young; again, I'm not. I hate everybody this evening."

"What's the matter? Has Nellie deserted you?"

"She? Not much. I had to tell her to go"—this with a joyless little laugh—"she quit work and wouldn't behave herself. So now I'm going on alone."

"And you won't go home?"

"Never in the world," she said with almost fierce energy; then some thought made her laugh in the same way as before. Howard decided that she had not told him everything about her home life, even though she had rattled on as if there were nothing to conceal. He sat watching her, she looking straight before her, her small bare hands clasped in her lap. He was pitying her keenly—this child, at once stunted and abnormally developed, this stray from one of the classes that keeps their women sheltered; and here she was adrift, without any of those resources of experience which assist the girls of the tenements.

Her features were small, sensitive, regular. Her eyes were brown with lines of reddish gold raying from the pupils. Her chin and mouth were firm enough, yet suggested weakness through the passions. Her clear skin had the glow of youth and health upon its smooth surface. She was certainly beautiful and she certainly had magnetism.

"What do you think is going to become of you?" he asked.

"I don't know," she said, after a deep sigh. "A girl doesn't have a fair chance. I don't seem to be able to have any fun without getting into trouble. I don't know what to think. It's all so black. I wish I was dead."

Her dreary tone put the deepest pathos into her words. Howard had seen despondency in youth before—had felt it himself. But there had always been a certain lightness in it. Here was a mere child who evidently thought, and thought with reason, that there was no hope for her ; and her despair was not a passing cloud or storm, but a settled conviction.

" There doesn't seem to be any chance for a young girl," she repeated as if that phrase summed up all that was weighing upon her. And Howard feared that she, was right. Even the readiest of all commodities, advice, failed him. " What can she do ? " he thought. " If she has no home, worth speaking of "—then he went on aloud :

" Haven't you friends ? "

She laughed again with that slight moving of the lips and with eyes mirthless. " Who wants me for a friend ? Nobody'd think I was respectable. And I guess I'm not so very. There's Nellie and her—friends. Oh, the girls join in with the men to drag other girls down. But I won't do that. I don't care what becomes of me—except that."

" Why ? " he asked, curious for her explanation of this aversion.

" I don't know why," she replied. " There doesn't seem to be any good reason. I've thought I would several times. And then—well, I just couldn't."

Howard turned the subject and tried to draw her out of this mood. They sat there for several hours and became well acquainted. He found that she had an intelligent way of looking at things, that she observed closely, and that she appreciated and understood far more than he had expected.

It was the beginning of a series of evenings spent together. He took her with him on many of his assignments and they often dined together at "Le Chat Noir" or the "Restaurant de Paris," or "The Manhattan" over in Second Avenue. Late in June she bought a new gown—a pale-grey with ribbons and hat to match. Howard was amused at the anxious expression in her gold-brown eyes as she waited for his opinion. And when he said: "Well, well, I never saw you look so pretty," she looked much prettier with a slight colour rising to tint the usual pallor of her cheeks.

One Sunday he came home in the afternoon and found her helping the maid at straightening his rooms. As he lay on the lounge smoking he watched her lazily. She handled his books with a great deal of awe. She opened one of them and sat on the floor in the childlike way she often had. She read several sentences aloud. It was a tangle of technical words on the subject of political economy.

"What do you have such stupid things around

for?" she said, smiling and rising. She began to arrange the books and papers on the table. He was looking at her but thinking of something else when he became conscious that she had got suddenly white to the lips. He jumped to his feet.

"What's the matter?" he asked, "are you going to faint?"

Her eyes were shining as with fever out of a ghostly face. Her lips trembled as she answered: "Oh it's nothing. I do this often." She went slowly into the back room where the maid was. In a few minutes she returned, apparently as usual. She flitted about uneasily, taking up now one thing, now another in a purposeless, nervous way.

"I never was in here before," she said. "You've got lots of pretty things. Whose picture is this?"

"That? Oh, my sister-in-law out in Chicago."

Howard did not then understand why she became so gay, why her eyes danced with happiness, why as soon as she went into the hall she began to sing and kept it up in her own room, quieting down only to burst forth again. He did not even especially note the swift change, the, for her, extraordinary mood of high spirits. It was about this time that their relations began to change.

Howard had thought of her, or had thought that he thought of her, only as a lonely and desolate child, to be taught so far as he was capable of teaching and she of learning. He was conscious of her extreme youth and of the impassable gulf of thought and taste between them. He did not take her feelings into account at all. It never occurred to him that this part of friend and patron which he was playing was not safe for him, not just and right toward her.

One night he took her to a ball at the Terrace Garden—a respectable, amusing affair "under the auspices of the Young-German-American-Shooting-Society." The next day a reporter for the *Sun* whom he knew slightly said to him with a grin he did not like: "Mighty pretty little girl you're taking about with you, Howard. Where'd you pick her up?"

Howard reddened, angry with himself for reddening, angry with the *Sun* man for his impudence, ashamed that he had put himself and Alice in such a position. But the incident brought the matter of his relation with her sharply and clearly before his mind and conscience.

"This must stop," he said to himself; "it must stop at once. It is unjust to her. And it is dragging me into an entanglement."

But the mischief had been done. She loved him. And with the confidence of youth and inexperience, she was disregarding all the obstacles, was giving herself up to the dream that he would presently love her in return, with the end as in the story books. Indeed love stories became her constant companions. Where she once read them for amusement, she now read them as a Christian reads his Bible—for instruction, inspiration, faith, hope and courage.

One evening in July—it was in the week of Independence Day—Howard's windows and door were thrown wide to get the full benefit of whatever stir there might be in the air. He was sprawled upon the lounge, the table drawn close and upon it a lamp shedding a dim light through the room but enough near by to let him read. He had dropped his book and was thinking whether a stroll in the Square in the moonlight would repay the trouble of moving. There were steps in the hall and then, peeping round the door-frame was the face of his young neighbour.

"Hello," he said, "I thought you were out somewhere. Come in."

"No, I'm going to bed," she answered, nevertheless gradually edging into the room. She was wearing a loose wrapper of flowered silk, somewhat worn and never very fine. Her black hair hung in a long thick braid to her waist and she looked even younger than usual.

"Where have you been all evening?" asked Howard.

"Oh, I've been up to see a friend. She lives in

Harlem, and she wants me to come and live with her."

"Are you going?" Howard inquired, noting that he was interested and not pleased. "The house wouldn't seem natural without you."

She gave him a quick, gratified glance and, advancing further into the room, sat upon the arm of the big rocking-chair. "She gave me a good talking to," she went on with a smile. "She told me I ought not to live alone at my age. She said I ought to live with her and meet some friends of hers. She said maybe I'd find a nice fellow to marry."

Howard thought over this as he smoked and at last said in an ostentatiously judicial tone: "Well, I think she's right. I don't see what else there is to do. You can't live on down here alone always. What's become of Nellie?"

"Nellie's got to be a bad girl," said Alice with a blush and a dropping of the eyes. "She's in Fourteenth Street every night. She says she doesn't care what happens to her. I saw her last night and she wanted me to come with her. She says it's of no use for me to put on airs. She says I've got no friends and I might as well join her sooner as later."

"Well?" Howard was keeping his eyes carefully away from hers.

"Oh, I sha'n't go with her. As long as a girl has

got anything at all to live for, she doesn't want that. Besides I'd rather go to the East River."

"Drowning's a serious matter," said Howard with a smile and with banter in his tone.

"Yes, it is," said the girl seriously, "I've thought of it. And I don't believe I could."

"Then you'd better go with your friend and get married."

"I don't want to get married," she replied, shaking her head slowly from side to side.

"That's what all the girls say," laughed Howard. "But of course you will. It's the only thing to do."

"Then why don't you get married?" asked Alice, tracing one of the flowers in her wrapper with her slim, brown forefinger.

"I couldn't if I would and I wouldn't if I could."

"Oh, you could get a nice girl to marry you, I'm sure," she said, the colour rising faintly toward her long, downcast lashes.

"But who would get the money? It takes money to keep a nice girl."

"Oh, not much," said Alice earnestly, yet with a queer hesitation in her voice. "You oughtn't to marry those extravagant girls. I've read about them and I think they don't make very good wives, real wives to save money and—and care."

"You seem to know a good deal about these things

for your age," said Howard, much amused and showing it.

"I don't care," she persisted, "you ought to get married."

Howard felt that this was the time to clear the girl's mind of any "notions" she might have got. He would be very clever, very adroit. He would not let her suspect that he had any idea of her thoughts. Indeed he was not perfectly certain that he had. But he would gently and frankly tell her the truth.

"I shall never get married," he said, sitting up and talking as one who is discussing a case which he understands thoroughly yet has no personal interest in. "I haven't the money and I haven't the desire. I am what they would call a confirmed bachelor. I wouldn't marry any girl who had not been brought up as I have been. We should be unhappy together unsuited each to the other. She would soon hate me. Besides, I wish to be free. I care more for freedom than I ever shall for any human being. As I am now, so I shall always be, a wandering fellow without ties. It is not a pleasant prospect for old age. But I have made up my mind to it and I shall never marry."

The girl's hands had dropped limp into her lap; her face was down so that he could barely see the burning blush which overspread it.

"You don't mean that," she said in a voice that was queer and choked.

"Oh yes, I do, little girl," he answered, intending to smile when she should look up.

When she did lift her eyes, his smile could not come. For her face was grey and her lips bloodless and from her eyes looked despair. Howard glanced away instantly. With rude hand he had suddenly toppled into the dust this child's dream-castle of love and happiness which he had himself helped her build. He felt like a criminal. But partly from a sense of duty, chiefly from the cowardice of self-preservation, he made no effort to lighten her suffering.

"I should only prolong it," he thought, "only make matters worse. "To-morrow—perhaps."

If she had been worldly wise, even if she had not been so completely absorbed in her worship of him that her woman-instincts were dormant, she would herself have found hope. But she had not a suspicion that these strong words of apparent finality were spoken to give himself courage, to keep him from obeying the impulse to respond to the appeal of her youth to his, her aloneness to his, her passion to his. She believed him literally.

There was a long silence. He heard her move, heard a suppressed cry and glanced toward her again.

She was darting from the room. A second later her door crashed. He started up and after her, hesitated, returned to his book--but not to his reading.

Toward noon the next day, he passed her room on his way out. The door was wide open; none of her belongings was in sight; the maid was sweeping energetically. She paused when she saw him.

"Miss Alice left this morning," she said, "and the room's been let to another party."

VI.

IN A BOHEMIAN QUICKSAND.

HOWARD could have got her new address; and for many weeks habit, at first steadily, afterward intermittently, teased him to look her up. He was amazed at her hold upon him. At times the longing for her was so intense that he almost suspected himself of being in love with her.

"I escaped from that none too soon," he congratulated himself. "It wasn't nearly so one-sided as I thought."

He had never been gregarious. Thus far he had not had a single intimate friend, man or woman. He knew many people and knew them well. They liked him and some of them sought his friendship. These were often puzzled because it was easy to get acquainted with him, impossible to know him intimately.

The explanation of this combination of openness and reserve, friendliness and unapproachableness, was that his boyhood and youth had been spent wholly among books. That life had trained him not to look to others for amusement, sympathy or counsel, but to depend upon himself. As his temperament was open and good-natured and sympathetic, he was as free from enemies and enmities as he was from friends and friendships.

Women there had been—several women, a succession of idealizations which had dispersed in the strong light of his common sense. He had never disturbed himself about morals in what he regarded as the limited sense. He always insisted that he was free ; and he was careful only of his personal pride and of taking no advantage of another. What he had said to Alice about marriage was true—as to his intentions, at least. A poor woman, he felt, he could not marry ; a rich woman, he felt, he would not marry. And he cared nothing about marriage because he was never lonely, never leaned or wished to lean upon another, abhorred the idea of any one leaning upon him ; because he regarded freedom as the very corner-stone of his scheme of life.

The nearest he had come to companionship was with Alice. With the other women whom he had known in various degrees from warmth to white-heat, there had been interruptions, no such constant freedom of access, no such intermingling of daily life. Her he had seen at all hours and in all circumstances. She never disturbed him but was ready to talk when he wished to listen, listened eagerly when he talked, and was silent and beautiful and restful to look at when he wished to indulge in the dissipation of mental laziness.

As she loved him, she showed him only the best that there was in her and showed it in the most attractive of all lights.

While he was still wavering or fancying that he was wavering, the Managing Editor sent him to "do" a great strike-riot in the coal regions of Pennsylvania. He was there for three weeks, active day and night, interested in the new phases of life—the mines and the miners, the display of fierce passions, the excitement, the peril.

When he returned to New York, Alice had ceased to tempt him.

* * * * * * * * *

One midnight in the early spring he was in his sitting room, reading and a little bored. There came a knock at the door. He hoped that it was some one bringing something interesting or coming to propose a search for something interesting. "Come in," he said with welcome in his voice. The door opened. It was Alice.

She was dressed much as she had been the first time he talked with her—a loose, clinging wrapper open at the throat. There was a change in her face—a change for the better but also for the worse. She looked more intelligent, more of a woman. There was more sparkle in her eyes and in her smile. But—Howard saw instantly the price she had paid. As the German had suggested, she had "got on up town."

She was pulling at the long broad blue ribbons of her negligee. Her hands were whiter and her pink finger nails had had careful attention. She smiled, enjoying his astonishment. "I have come back," she said.

Howard came forward and took her hand. "I'm glad, very glad to see you. For a minute I thought I was dreaming."

"Yes," she went on, "I'm in my old room. I came this afternoon. I must have been asleep, for I didn't hear you come in."

"I hope it isn't bad luck that has flung you back here."

"Oh, no. I've been doing very well. I've been saving up to come. And when I had enough to last me through the summer, I—I came."

"You've been at work?"

She dropped her eyes and flushed. And her fingers played more nervously with her ribbons.

"You needn't treat me as a child any longer," she said at last in a low voice; "I'm eighteen now and—well, I'm not a child."

Again there was a long pause. Howard, watching

her downcast face, saw her steadying her expression to meet his eyes. When she looked, it was straight at him—appeal but also defiance.

"I don't ask anything of you," she said, "we are both free. And I wanted to see you. I was sick of all those others—up there. I've never had—had—this out of my mind. And I've come. And I can see you sometimes. I won't be in the way."

Howard went over to the window and stared out into the lights and shadows of the leafy Square. When he turned again she had lighted and was smoking one of his cigarettes.

"Well," he said smiling down at her, "Why not? Put on a street gown and we'll go out and get supper and talk it over."

She sprang up, her face alight. She was almost running toward the door. Midway she stopped, turned and came slowly back. She put one of her arms upon his shoulder—a slender, cool, smooth, white arm with the lace of the wide sleeve slipping away from it. She turned her face up until her mouth, like a rosebud, was very near his lips. There was appeal in her eyes.

"I'm very, very glad to see you," Howard said as he kissed her.

* * * * * * * * *

And so Howard's life was determined for the next four years.

He worked well at his profession. He read a great deal. He wrote fiction and essays in desultory fashion and got a few things printed in the magazines. He led a life that was a model of regularity. But he knew the truth—that Alice had ended his career.

He was content. Ambition had always been vague with him and now his habit of following the line of least resistance had drifted him into this mill-pond. Sometimes he would give himself up to bitter self-reproach, disgusted that he should be so satisfied, so non-resisting in a lot in every way the reverse of that which he had marked out for himself. If he had been chained he might, probably would, have broken away. But Alice never attempted to control him. His will was her law. She was especially shrewd about money matters, so often the source of disputes and estrangements. Two months after she reappeared, she proposed that they take an apartment together.

"I saw one to-day in West Twelfth Street at seventy dollars a month," she said, "and I'm sure I could manage it so that you would be much better off than you are now."

He viewed this plan with suspicion. It definitely committed him to a mode of life which he had always regarded as degrading both to the man and the woman and as certain of a calamitous ending. So he made excuses for delay, fully intending never to yield. But although Alice did not speak of her plan again, he found himself more and more attracted by it, caught himself speculating about various apartments he happened to see as he went about the streets. She must have been conscious of what was going on in his mind; for when, a month after she had spoken, he said abruptly: "Where was that apartment you saw?" she went straight on discussing the details as if there had been no interval. She was ready to act.

The apartment was taken in her name—Mrs. Cammack, the "Mrs." being necessary to account for him. They selected the furniture together, he as interested as she and very pleased to find that she had the same good taste in those matters that she had in dress. She took all the troubles and annoyances upon herself. When she invited him to assist in the arrangement, it was in matters that amused him and at times when she was sure he had nothing else to do. It is not strange that he got a wholly false idea of the difficulties of setting up an establishment.

After a month of selecting and discussing, of pleasure in the new experience, pleasure in Alice's enthusiasm and excitement and happiness, he found himself master of five attractive and comfortable rooms, his clothing, his books, all his belongings properly arranged. The door was opened for him by a cleanlooking coloured maid, with a tiny white cap on her head.

As he looked around and then at the beautiful face with the wistful, gold-brown eyes so anxiously following his wandering glance, he was very near to loving her. Indeed, he was like a husband who has left out that period of passionate love which extends into married life until it gives place to boredom, or to dislike, or to some such sympathetic affection as he felt for Alice. "It is just this that holds me," he thought, in his infrequent moods of dissatisfaction. "If we quarrelled or if there were any deep feeling on my side, I should not be in this mess. I should be"— Well, where would he be? "Probably worse off," he usually added.

Certainly he could not have been freer, for she never questioned him; and, if she was ever uneasy or jealous when he came in late—for him—without telling her where he had been, she never showed it. She had no friends, and he often wondered how she passed the time when he was not with her. Whenever he inquired he got the same answer: She had been busying herself with their home; she had been planning to save money or to make him more comfortable; she had been reading to improve her mind and to enable herself to start him talking on subjects that interested him.

No matter how unexpectedly he looked in upon her life or her mind, he found—himself.

One day she said to him—it was after two years of this life: "Something is worrying you. Is it about me? You look at me so queerly at times."

"Yes," he answered. "It is about you. Tell me, Miss Black-Hair, do you never think of getting old?"

"No," she smiled. "I shall wait until I am twenty-five before I begin to think of that."

"But don't you see that this sort of thing must stop sometime? It is unjust to you. When I think of it, I reproach myself for permitting us to get into it."

"I am happy," she said, looking straight at him, terror in her eyes.

"But you have no friends?"

"Who has? And what do I want with friends?"

"But don't you see, I can't introduce you to anybody. I can't talk about you to the people I know. I am always having to explain you away, always having to act as if I were ashamed of this, my real life. At times I am Anglo-Saxon enough to be really ashamed of it. And I ought to be and am ashamed of myself."

"Don't let's talk about it. You and I understand. Why should we bother about the rest of the world?"

"No, we *must* talk about it. I have been going over it carefully. We must—must be married."

He laid his hand upon hers. She blushed deeply and lowered her head. A tear dropped upon the front of her gown and hung glittering in the meshes of the white lace. She crept into his arms and buried her face upon his shoulder and sobbed. He had never seen her even look like tears before.

"We must be married," he repeated, patting her on the shoulder.

She shook her head in negation.

"Yes," he said firmly, mentally noting that this was the very first time he had ever caught her in a pretense.

"No." Her tone was as firm as his. She lifted her head and put her cheek against his. "It makes me very proud that you ask it. But—I—I do not——"

"Do not—what?"

"I do not want—I will not—risk losing you."

"But you won't lose me. You will have me more than ever."

"Some men—yes. But not you."

"And why not I, O Wisdom?"

"Because—because—do you think I have watched you all this time, without learning something about you? The way to keep you is to leave you free. I do not want your name. I do not want your friends I do not want to be respectable. I want—just you."

"But are we not as good as married now?"

"Yes—that's it. And I want it to keep on. I never cared for anybody until I saw you. I shall never care for anybody else. I never shall try. I want you as long as I can have you. And then——"

"And then," Howard laughed or rather, pretended to laugh, "and then, 'Oh, dig me a grave both wide and deep, wide and deep.' How like twenty-years-old that is."

She seemed not to hear his jest and presently went on: "Do you remember the evening before I left, down there at Mrs. Sands's?"

"The night you proposed to me?" Howard said, pulling her ear.

She smiled faintly and continued: "I thought it all out that night. I intended to come back just as I did. I went deliberately. I——"

Howard put his hand over her lips.

"O, I am not going to tell anything," said she, evading his fingers. "Only this—that I understood you then, understood just why you would never marry. Not so clearly as I understand it now, but still I—understood. And you have been teaching me ever since, teaching me manners, teaching me how to read and think and talk. And more than all, you've taught me your way of looking at life."

Howard held her away from him and studied her face, surprise in his eyes. "Isn't it strange?" he said.

"Here I've been seeing you day after day all this time, have had a chance to know you better than I ever knew any one in my life, have had you very near to me day and night. And just now, as I look at you, I see the real you for the first time in two years."

"I have been wondering when you would look at me again," said Alice with a small, sly smile.

"Why, you are a woman grown. Where is the little girl I knew, the little girl who used to look up to me?"

"Oh, she's gone these two years. She proposed to you and, when you refused her, she—died."

"Yes—we must be married," Howard went on. "Why not? It is more convenient, let us say."

Alice shook her head and put her cheek against his again and clasped his fingers in hers. "No, my instinct is against it. Some day—perhaps. But not now, not now. I want you. I want only you. We are together out here—out beyond the pale. Inside, others would come in and—and surely come between us. I want no others—none."

VII.

A LITTLE CANDLE GOES OUT.

HOWARD was now thirty years old. Park Row had long ceased talking of him as a "coming man." While his style of writing was steadily improving, he wrote with no fixed aim, wrote simply for the day, for the newspaper which dies with the day of its date. Some of his acquaintances wondered why a man of such ability should thus stand still. The less observant spoke of him as an impressive example of the "journalistic blight." Those who looked deeper saw the truth—a dangerous facility, a perilous inertia, a fatal entanglement. Facility enabled him to earn a good living with ease, working as he chose. Inertia prevented him from seeking opportunities for advancement. Entanglement shut him off from the men and women of his own kind who would have thrust opportunities upon him and compelled him.

Howard himself saw this clearly in his occasional moods of self-criticism. But as he saw no remedy, he raged intermittently and briefly, and straightway relapsed. Vanity supplied him with many excuses and consolations. Was he not one of the best reporters in the profession? Where was there another, where indeed in any profession were there many of his age, making five thousand a year? Was he not always improving his mind? Was he not more and more careful in his personal habits? Was he not respected by all who knew him; looked upon as a successful man; regarded by those with whom he came in daily contact as a leader in the profession, a model for style, a marvel for facility and versatility and for the quantity of good "copy" he could turn out in a brief time? But with all the soothings of vanity he never could quite hide from himself that his life was a failure up to that moment.

"Why try to lie to myself?" he thought. "It's never a question of what one has done but always of what one could have and should have done. I am thirty and I have been marking time for at least four years. Preparing by study and reading? Yes, but not preparing for anything."

On the whole he was glad that Alice had refused to marry him. Her reason was valid. But there was another which he thought she did not see. He was deceived as to the depth of her insight because he did not watch her closely. He had no suspicion how many, many times, in their moments of demonstrativeness, she listened for those words which never came, listened and turned away to hide from him the disappointment in her eyes.

He did not love her--and she knew it. She did not inspire ambition in him—and she knew it. She simply kept him comfortable and contented. She simply prevented his amatory instincts from gathering strength vigorously to renew that search which men and women keep up incessantly until they find what they seek. She knew this also but never permitted herself to see it clearly.

He was pleased with her but not proud of her. He was not exactly ashamed of his relation with her but—well, he never relaxed his precautions for keeping it conventionally concealed. He still had a room at his club and occupied it occasionally. He laughed at himself, despised himself in a gentle, soothing way. But he excused himself to himself with earnestness despite his sarcasms at his own expense. And for the most of the time he was content—so well, so comfortably content that if his mind had not been so nervously active he would have taken on the form and look of settled middle-life.

There was just the one saving quality—his mental alertness. All his life he had had insatiable intellectual curiosity. It had kept him from wasting his time at play when he was a boy. It had kept him from plunging deeply into dissipation when youth was hot in his veins. It was now keeping him from the sluggard's fate.

* * * * * * * * *

On the last day of January—six weeks after his thirtieth birthday—he came home earlier than usual, as they were going to the theatre and were to dine at seven. He found Alice in bed and the doctor sitting beside her.

"You'll have to get some one else to go with you, I'm afraid," she said with good-humoured resignation, a trifle over-acted. "My cold is worse and the doctor says I must stay in bed."

"Nothing serious?" Howard asked anxiously, for her cheeks were flaming.

"Oh, no. Just the cold. And I am taking care of myself."

He accompanied the doctor to the door of the apartment. At the threshold the doctor whispered: "Make some excuse and come to my office. I wish to see you particularly."

He grew pale. "Don't let her see," urged the doctor. He went back to Alice, sick at heart. "I must go out and arrange for some one else to do the play for me," he said. "I shall spend the evening with you."

She protested, but faintly. He went to the doctor's office.

"She must go south at once," he began, after looking at Howard steadily and keenly. "Nothing can save her life. That may prolong it."

Howard seemed not to understand.

"She must go to-morrow or she'll be gone forever in ten days."

"Impossible," Howard said in a dull, dazed tone.

"At once, I tell you—at once."

"Impossible," Howard repeated. He was saying to himself, "And only this afternoon I wished I were free and wondered how I could free myself." He laughed strangely.

"Impossible," he said again. And again he laughed. The room swam around. He stood up. "Impossible!" he said a fourth time, almost shouting it. And he struck the doctor full in the face, reeled and fell headlong to the floor. When he recovered consciousness he was lying on a lounge, the doctor's assistant standing beside him.

"I must go to her," he exclaimed and sat up. He saw the doctor a few feet away, holding a cloth odorous of arnica to his cheek. Howard remembered and began, "I beg your pardon,"—The doctor interrupted with: "Not at all. I've had many queer experiences but never one like that." But Howard had ceased to hear. He was staring vacantly at the floor, repeating to himself, "And I wished to be free. And I am to be free."

"You must go back to her. Take her south to-morrow. Asheville is the best place."

Howard was on his way to the door. "We shall go by the first train," he said.

"Pardon me for telling you so abruptly," said the doctor, following him. "But I saw that you weren't—that is I couldn't help noticing that you and she were—And usually the man in such cases—well, my sympathy is for the woman."

"Do you think a man voluntarily lives with a woman because he hates her?" Howard asked, with an angry sneer. He bowed coldly and was gone.

As he looked at Alice he saw that it was of no use to try to deceive her. "We must go South in the morning," he almost whispered, taking her hand and kissing it again and again, slowly and gently.

The next day but one they were at Asheville and two weeks later Howard could not hide from himself that she would soon be gone.

* * * * * * * * *

Her bed was drawn up to the open window and she was propped with pillows. A mild breeze was flooding the room with the odours of the pine forests and the gardens. She looked out, dilated her nostrils and her eyes.

"Beautiful!" she murmured. "It is so easy to die here."

She put out her hand and laid it in his.

"I want you, my Alice." He was looking into her eyes and she into his. "I need you. I can't do without you."

She smiled with an expression of happiness. "Is it wrong," she asked, "to take pleasure in another's pain? I see that you are in pain, that you suffer. And, oh, it makes me happy, so happy."

"Don't," he begged. "Please don't."

"But listen," she went on. "Don't you see why? Because I—because I love you. There," she was smiling again. "I promised myself I never, never would say it first. And I've broken my word."

"What do you mean?"

"For nearly four years—all the years I've really lived—I have had only one thought—my love for you. But I never would say it, never would say 'I love you,' because I knew that you did not love me."

He was beginning to speak but she lifted her hand to his lips. Then she put it back in his and pushed her fingers up his coat-sleeve until they were hidden, resting upon his bare arm.

"No, you did not." Her voice was low and the words came slowly. "But since we came here, you have loved me. If I were to get well, were to go back, you would not. Ah, if you knew, if you only knew how I have wanted your love, how I have lain awake night after night, hour after hour, whispering under my breath 'I love you. I love you. Why do you not love me?'"

Howard put his head down so that his face was hid from her in her lap.

"After the doctor had talked to me a few minutes, had asked me a few questions," she went on, "I knew. And I was not sorry. It was nearly over, anyhow, dear. Did you know it? I often wondered if you did. Yes, I saw many little signs. I wouldn't admit it to myself until this illness came. Then I confessed it to myself. And I was not sorry we were to part this way. But I did not expect"—and she drew a long breath—"happiness!"

"No, no," he protested, lifting his face and looking at her. She drank in the expression of his eyes—the love, the longing, the misery—as if it had been a draught of life.

"Ah, you make me so happy, so happy. How much I owe to you. Four long, long, beautiful years. How much! How much! And at last—love!"

There was silence for several minutes. Then he spoke: "I loved you from the first, I believe. Only I never appreciated you. I was so self-absorbed. And you—you fed my vanity, never insisted upon yourself."

"But we have had happiness. And no one, no one, no one will ever be to you what I have been."

"I love you." Howard's voice had a passionate earnestness in it that carried conviction. "The light goes out with you."

"With this little candle? No, no, dear—*my* dear. You will be a great man. You will not forget; but you will go on and do the things that I'm afraid I didn't help, maybe hindered, you in trying to do. And you will keep a little room in your heart, a very little room. And I shall be in there. And you'll open the door every once in a while and come in and take me in your arms and kiss me. And I think—yes, I feel that—that I shall know and thrill."

Her voice sank lower and lower and then her eyes closed, and presently he called the nurse.

The next day he rose from his bed, just at the connecting door between his room and hers, and looked in at her. The shades were drawn and only a faint light crept into the room. He thought he saw her stir and went nearer.

"Why, they've made you very gay this morning," he laughed, "with the red ribbons at your neck."

There was no answer. He came still nearer. The red ribbons were long streamers of blood. She was dead.

VIII.

A STRUGGLE FOR SELF-CONTROL.

HE left her at Asheville as she wished—"where I have been happiest and where I wish you to think of me." On the train coming north he reviewed his past and made his plans for the future.

As to the past he had only one regret—that he had not learned to appreciate Alice until too late. He felt that his failure to advance had been due entirely to himself—to his inertia, his willingness to seize any pretext for refraining from action. As to the future—work, work with a purpose. His mind must be fully and actively occupied. There must be no leisure, for leisure meant paralysis.

At the Twenty-third Street ferry-house he got into a hansom and gave the address of "the flat." He did not note where he was until the hansom drew up at the curb. He leaned forward and looked at the house—at their windows with the curtains which she had draped so gracefully, which she and he had selected at Vantine's one morning. How often he had seen her standing between those curtains, looking out for him, her blue-black hair waving back from her forehead so beautifully and her face ready to smile so soon as ever she should catch sight of him.

He leaned back and closed his eyes. The blood was pounding through his temples and his eyeballs seemed to be scalding under the lids.

"Never again," he moaned. "How lonely it is."

The cabman lifted the trap. "Here we are, sir."

"Yes—in a moment." Where should he go? But what did it matter? "To a hotel," he said. "The nearest."

"The Imperial?"

"That will do—yes—go there."

He resolved never to return to "the flat." On the following day he sent for the maid and arranged the breaking up. He gave her everything except his personal belongings and a few of Alice's few possessions—those he could keep, and those which he must destroy because he could not endure the thought of any one having them.

At the office all understood his mourning; but no one, not even Kittredge, knew him well enough to intrude beyond gentler looks and tones. Kittredge had written a successful novel and was going abroad for two years of travel and writing. Howard took his rooms in the Royalton. They dined together a few nights before he sailed.

"And now," said Kittredge, "I'm my own master. Why, I can't begin to fill the request for 'stuff.' I can go where I please, do as I please. At last I shall work. For I don't call the drudgery done under compulsion work."

"Work!" Howard repeated the word several times absently. Then he leaned forward and said with what was for him an approach to the confidential: "What a mess I have been making of my life! What waste! What folly! I've behaved like a child, an impulsive, irresponsible child. And now I must get to work, really to work."

"With your talents a year or so of work would free you."

"Oh, I'm free." Howard hesitated and flushed. "Yes, I'm free," he repeated bitterly. "We are all free except for the shackles we fasten upon ourselves and can unlock for ourselves. I don't agree with you that earning one's daily bread is drudgery."

"Well, let's see you work—work for something definite. Why don't you try for some higher place on the paper—correspondent at Washington or London—no, not London, for that is a lounging job which would ruin even an energetic man. Why not try for the editorial staff? They ought to have somebody upstairs who takes an interest in something besides politics."

"But doesn't a man have to write what he doesn't believe? You know how Segur is always laughing at the protection editorials he writes, although he is a free-trader."

"Oh, there must be many directions in which the paper is free to express honest opinions."

Howard began that very night. As soon as he reached his club where he was living for a few days he sat down to the file of the *News-Record* and began to study its editorial style and method. He had learned a great deal before three o'clock in the morning and had written a short editorial on a subject he took from the news. In the morning he read his article again and decided that with a few changes—adjectives cut out, long sentences cut up, short sentences made shorter and the introduction and the conclusion omitted—it would be worth handing in. With the corrected article in his hand he knocked at the door of the editor's room.

It was a small, plainly furnished office—no carpet, three severe chairs, a revolving book case with a battered and dusty bust of Lincoln on it, a table strewn with newspaper cuttings. Newspapers from all parts of the world were scattered about the floor. At the table sat the editor, Mr. Malcolm, whom Howard had never before seen.

He was short and slender, with thin white hair and

a smooth, satirical face, deeply wrinkled and unhealthily pale. He was dressed in black but wore a string tie of a peculiarly lively shade of red. His most conspicuous feature was his nose—long, narrow, pointed, sarcastic.

"My name is Howard," began the candidate, all but stammering before Mr. Malcolm's politely uninterested glance, "and I come from downstairs."

"Oh—so you are Mr. Howard. I've heard of you often. Will you be seated?"

"Thank you—no. I've only brought in a little article I thought I'd submit for your page. I'd like to write for it and, if you don't mind, I'll bring in an article occasionally."

"Glad to have it. We like new ideas; and a new pen, a new mind, ought to produce them. If you don't see your articles in the paper, you'll know what has happened to them. If you do, paste them on space slips and send them up by the boy on Thursdays." Mr. Malcolm nodded and smiled and dipped his pen in the ink-well.

The editorial appeared just as Howard wrote it. He read and reread it, admiring the large, handsome editorial type in which it was printed, and deciding that it was worthy of the excellent place in the column which Mr. Malcolm had given it. He wrote another that very day and sent it up by the boy. He found it in his desk the next noon with "Too abstract—never forget that you are writing for a newspaper" scrawled across the last page in blue pencil.

In the two following months Howard submitted thirty-five articles. Three were published in the main as he wrote them, six were "cut" to paragraphs, one appeared as a letter to the editor with "H" signed to it. The others disappeared. It was not encouraging, but Howard kept on. He knew that if he stopped marching steadily, even though hopelessly, toward a definite goal, a heavy hand would be laid upon his shoulder to drag him away and fling him down upon a grave.

As it was, desperately though he fought to refrain from backward glances, he was now and again taken off his guard. A few of her pencil marks on the margin of a leaf in one of his books; a gesture, a little mannerism of some woman passing him in the street—and he would be ready to sink down with weariness and loneliness, like a tired traveller in a vast desert.

He completely lost self-control only once. It was a cold, wet May night and everything had gone against him that day. He looked drearily round his rooms as he came in. How stiff, how forbidding, how desert they seemed! He threw himself into a big chair.

"No friends," he thought, "no one that cares a rap whether I live or die, suffer or am happy. Nothing to care for. Why do I go on? What's the use if one has not an object—a human object?"

And their life together came flooding back—her eyes, her kisses, her attentions, her passionate love for him, so pervasive yet so unobtrusive; the feeling of her smooth, round arm about his neck; her way of pressing close up to him and locking her fingers in his; the music of her voice, singing her heartsong to him yet never putting it into words——

He stumbled over to the divan and stretched himself out and buried his face in the cushions. "Come back!" he sobbed. "Come back to me, dear." And then he cried, as a man cries—without tears, with sobs choking up into his throat and issuing in moans.

"Curious," he said aloud when the storm was over and he was sitting up, ashamed before himself for his weakness, "who would have suspected me of this?"

IX.

AMBITION AWAKENS.

HOWARD was now thirty-two. He was still trying for the editorial staff; but in the last month only five of his articles had been printed to twenty-three thrown away. A national campaign was coming on and the *News-Record* was taking a political stand that seemed to him sound and right. For the first time he tried political editorials.

The cause aroused his passion for justice, for democratic equality and the abolition of privilege. He had something to say and he succeeded in saying it vigorously, effectively, with clearness and moderation of statement. How to avoid hysteria; how to set others on fire instead of only making of himself a fiery spectacle; how to be earnest, yet calm; how to be satirical yet sincere; how to be interesting, yet direct —these were his objects, pursued with incessant toiling, rewriting again and again, recasting of sentences, careful balancing of words for exact shades of meaning.

"I shall never learn to write," had been his complaint of himself to himself for years. And in these days it seemed to him that he was farther from a good style than ever. His standards had risen, were rising; he feared that his power of accomplishment was failing. Therefore his heart sank and his face paled when an office boy told him that Mr. Malcolm wished to see him.

"I suppose it's to tell me not to annoy him with any more of my attempts," he thought. "Well, anyway, I've had the benefit of the work. I'll try a novel next."

"Take a seat," said Mr. Malcolm with an absent nod. "Just a moment, if you please."

On a chair beside him was the remnant of what had been a huge up-piling of newspapers—the exchanges that had come in during the past twenty-four hours. The Exchange Editor had been through them and Mr. Malcolm was reading "to feel the pulse of the country" and also to make sure that nothing of importance had been overlooked.

On the floor were newspapers by the score, thrown about tumultuously. Mr. Malcolm would seize a paper from the unread heap, whirl it open and send his glance and his long pointed nose tearing down one column and up another, and so from page to page. It took less than a minute for him to finish and fling away great sixteen page dailies. A few seconds sufficed for the smaller papers. Occasionally he took his long shears and with a skilful twist cut out a piece from the middle of a page and laid it and the shears upon the table with a single motion.

"Now, Mr. Howard." Malcolm sent the last paper to increase the chaos on the floor and faced about in his revolving chair. "How would you like to come up here?"

Howard looked at him in amazement. "You mean——"

"We want you to join the editorial staff. Mr. Walker has married him a rich wife and is going abroad to do literary work, which means that he is going to do nothing. Will you come?"

"It is what I have been working for."

"And very hard you have worked." Mr. Malcolm's cold face relaxed into a half-friendly, half-satirical smile. "After you'd been sending up articles for a fortnight, I knew you'd make it. You went about it systematically. An intelligent plan, persisted in, is hard to beat in this world of laggards and hap-hazard strugglers."

"And I was on the point of giving up—that is, giving up this particular ambition," Howard confessed.

"Yes, I saw it in your articles—a certain pessimism and despondency. You show your feelings plainly, young man. It is an excellent quality—but dangerous. A man ought to make his mind a machine working evenly without regard to his feelings or physical condition. The night my oldest child died—I was editor of a country newspaper—I wrote my leaders as usual. I never had written better. You can be absolute master inside, if you will. You can learn to use your feelings when they're helpful and to shut them off when they hinder."

"But don't you think that temperament——"

"Temperament—that's one of the subtlest forms of self-excuse. However, the place is yours. The salary is a hundred and twenty-five a week—an advance of about twelve hundred a year, I believe, on your average downstairs. Can you begin soon?"

"Immediately," said Howard, "if the City Editor is satisfied."

An office boy showed him to his room—a mere hole-in-the-wall with just space for a table-desk, a small table, a case of shelves for books of reference, and two chairs. The one window overlooked the lower end of Manhattan Island—the forest of business buildings peaked with the Titan-tenements of financial New York. Their big, white plumes of smoke and steam were waving in the wind and reflecting in pale pink the crimson of the setting sun.

Howard had his first taste of the intoxication of triumph, his first deep inspiration of ambition. He recalled his arrival in New York, his timidity, his dread lest he should be unable to make a living—

"Poor boy," they used to say at home, "he will have to be supported. He is too much of a dreamer." He remembered his explorations of those now familiar streets—how acutely conscious he had been that they were paved with stone, walled with stone, roofed with a stony sky, peopled with faces and hearts of stone. How miserably insignificant he had felt!

And all these years he had been almost content to be one of the crowd, like them exerting himself barely enough to provide himself with the essentials of existence. Like them, he had given no real thought to the morrow. And now, with comparatively little labour, he had put himself in the way to become a master, a director of the enormous concentrated energies summed up in the magic word New York.

The key to the situation was—work, incessant, self-improving, self-developing. "And it is the key to happiness also," he thought. "Work and sleep—the two periods of unconsciousness of self—are the two periods of happiness."

His aloofness freed him from the temptations of distraction. He knew no women. He did not put himself in the way of meeting them. He kept away from theatres. He sunk himself in a routine of labour which, viewed from the outside, seemed dull and monotonous. Viewed from his stand-point of acquisition, of achievement, it was just the reverse.

The mind soon adapts itself to and enjoys any mental routine which exercises it. The only difficulty is in forming the habit of the routine.

Howard was greatly helped by his natural bent toward editorial writing. The idea of discussing important questions each day with a vast multitude as an audience stirred his imagination and aroused his instincts for helping on the great world-task of elevating the race. This enthusiasm pleased and also amused his cynical chief.

"You believe in things?" Malcolm said to him after they had become well acquainted. "Well, it is an admirable quality—but dangerous. You will need careful editing. Your best plan is to give yourself up to your belief while you are writing—then to edit yourself in cold blood. That is the secret of success, of great success in any line, business, politics, a profession—enthusiasm, carefully revised and edited."

"It is difficult to be cold blooded when one is in earnest."

"True," Malcolm answered, "and there is the danger. My own enthusiasms are confined to the important things—food, clothing and shelter. It seems to me that the rest is largely a matter of taste, training and time of life. But don't let me discourage you. I only suggest that you may have to guard against believing so intensely that you produce the impression of being an impracticable, a fanatic. Be cautious always; be especially cautious when you are cocksure you're right. Unadulterated truth always arouses suspicion in the unaccustomed public. It has the alarming tastelessness of distilled water."

Howard was acute enough to separate the wisdom from the cynicism of his chief. He saw the lesson of moderation. "You have failed, my very able chief," he said to himself, "because you have never believed intensely enough to move you to act. You have attached too much importance to the adulteration—the folly and the humbug. And here you are, still only a critic, destructive but never constructive."

At first his associates were much amused by his intensity. But as he learned to temper and train his enthusiasm they grew to respect both his ability and his character. Before a year had passed they were feeling the influence of his force—his trained, informed mind, made vigorous by principles and ideals.

Malcolm had the keen appreciation of a broad mind for this honest, intelligent energy. He used the editorial "blue-pencil" for alteration and condensation with the hand of a master. He cut away Howard's crudities, toned down and so increased his intensity, and pointed it with the irony and satire necessary to make it carry far and penetrate easily.

Malcolm was at once giving Howard a reputation

greater than he deserved and training him to deserve it.

* * * * * * * * *

In the office next to Howard's sat Segur, a bachelor of forty-five who took life as a good-humoured jest and amused his leisure with the New Yorkers who devote a life of idleness to a nervous flight from boredom. Howard interested Segur who resolved to try to draw him out of his seclusion.

"I'm having some people to dinner at the Waldorf on Thursday," he said, looking in at the door. "Won't you join us?"

"I'd be glad to," replied Howard, casting about for an excuse for declining. "But I'm afraid I'd ruin your dinner. I haven't been out for years. I've been too busy to make friends or, rather, acquaintances."

"A great mistake. You ought to see more of people."

"Why? Can they tell me anything that I can't learn from newspapers or books more accurately and without wasting so much time? I'd like to know the interesting people and to see them in their interesting moments. But I can't afford to hunt for them through the wilderness of nonentities and wait for them to become interesting."

"But you get amusement, relaxation. Then too, it's first-hand study of life."

"I'm not sure of that. Yawning is not a very attractive kind of relaxation, is it? And as for study of life, eight years of reporting gave me more of that than I could assimilate. And it was study of realities, not of pretenses. As I remember them, 'respectable' people are all about the same, whether in their vices or in their virtues. They are cut from a few familiar, 'old reliable' patterns. No, I don't think there is much to be learned from respectability on dress parade."

"You'll be amused on Thursday. You must come. I'm counting on you."

Howard accepted—cordially as he could not refuse decently. Yet he had a presentiment or a shyness or an impatience at the interruption of his routine which reproached him for accepting with insistence and persistence.

X.

THE ETERNAL MASCULINE.

It was the first week in November, and in those days "everybody" did not stay in the country so late as now. There were many New Yorkers in the crowd of out-of-town people at the Waldorf. Howard was attracted, fascinated by the scene—carefully-groomed men and women, the air of gaiety and ease, the flowers, the music, the lights, the perfumes. At a glance it seemed a dream of life with evil and sorrow and pain banished.

"No place for a working man," thought he, "at least not for my kind of a working man. It appeals too sharply to the instincts for laziness and luxury."

He was late and stood in the entrance to the palm-garden, looking about for Segur. Soon he saw him waving from a table near the wall under the music-alcove.

"The oysters are just coming," said Segur. "Sit over there between Mrs. Carnarvon and Miss Trevor. They are cousins, Howard, so be cautious what you say to one about the other. Oh, here is Mr. Berersford."

The others knew each other well; Howard knew them only as he had seen their names in the "fashionable intelligence" columns of the newspapers. Mrs. Carnarvon was a small thin woman in a black velvet gown which made her thinness obtrusive and attractive or the reverse according as one's taste is toward or away from attenuation. Her eyes were a dull, greenish grey, her skin brown and smooth and tough from much exposure in the hunting field. Her cheeks were beginning to hang slightly, so that one said: "She is pretty, but she will soon not be." Her mouth proclaimed strong appetites—not unpleasantly since she was good-looking.

Miss Trevor was perhaps ten years younger than her cousin, not far from twenty-four. She had a critical, almost amused yet not unpleasant way of looking out of unusually clear blue-green eyes. Her hair was of an ordinary shade of dark brown, but fine and thick and admirably arranged to set off her long, sensitive, high bred features. Her chin and mouth expressed decision and strong emotions.

There was a vacant chair between Segur and Berersford and it was presently filled by a fat, middle-aged woman, neither blonde nor brunette, with a large, serene face. Upon it was written a frank confession that she had never in her life had an original thought capable of creating a ripple of interest. She was

Mrs. Sidney, rich, of an "old" family—in the New York meaning of the word "old"—both by marriage and by birth, much courted because of her position and because she entertained a great deal both in town and at a large and hospitable country house.

The conversation was lively and amused, or seemed to amuse, all. It was purely personal—about Kittie and Nellie and Jim and Peggie and Amy and Bob; about the sayings and doings of a few dozen people who constituted the intimates of these five persons.

Mrs. Carnarvon turned to the silent Howard at last and began about the weather.

"Horrible in the city, isn't it?"

"Well, perhaps it is," replied Howard. "But I fancied it delightful. You see I have not lived anywhere but New York for so long that I am hardly capable to judge."

"Why everybody says we have the worst climate in the world."

"Far be it from me to contradict everybody. But for me New York has the ideal climate. Isn't it the best of any great city in the world? You see, we have the air of the sea in our streets. And when the sun shines, which it does more days in the year than in any other great city, the effect is like champagne—or rather, like the effect champagne looks as if it ought to have."

"I hate champagne," said Mrs. Carnarvon. "Marian, you must not drink it; you know you mustn't." This to Miss Trevor who was lifting the glass to her lips. She drank a little of the champagne, then set the glass down slowly.

"What you said made me want to drink it," she said to Howard. "I was glad to hear your lecture on the weather. I had never thought of it before, but New York really has a fine climate. And only this afternoon I let that stupid Englishman—Plymouth—you've met him? No?—Well, at any rate, he was denouncing our climate and for the moment I forgot about London."

"Frightful there, isn't it, after October and until May?"

"Yes, and the air is usually stale even in the late spring. When it's warm, it's sticky. And when it's cold, it's raw."

"You are a New Yorker?"

"Yes," said Miss Trevor faintly, and for an instant showing surprise at his ignorance. "That is, I spend part of the winter here—like all New Yorkers."

"All?"

"Oh, all except those who don't count, or rather, who merely count."

"How do you mean?" Howard was taking advantage of her looking into her plate to smile with a suggestion of irony. She happened to glance up and so caught him.

"Oh," she said, smiling with frank irony at him, "I mean all those people—the masses, I think they're called—the people who have to be fussed over and reformed and who keep shops and—and all that."

"The people who work, you mean?"

"No, I mean the people you never meet about anywhere, the people who read the newspapers and come to the basement door."

"Oh, yes, I understand." Howard was laughing. "Well, that's one way of looking at life. Of course it's not my way."

"What is your way?"

"Why, being one of those who count only in the census, I naturally take a view rather different from yours. Now I should say that *your* people don't count. You see, I am most deeply interested in people who read newspapers."

"Oh, you write for the papers, like Jim Segur? What do you write?"

"What they call editorials."

"You are an editor?"

"Yes and no. I am one of the editors who does not edit but is edited."

"It must be interesting," said Miss Trevor, vaguely.

"More interesting than you imagine. But then

all work is that. In fact work is the only permanently interesting thing in life. The rest produces dissatisfaction and regret."

"Oh, I'm not so very dissatisfied. Yet I don't work."

"Are you quite sure? Think how hard you work at being fitted for gowns, at going about to dinners and balls and the like, at chasing foxes and anise seed bags and golf balls."

"But that is not work. It is amusing myself."

"Yes, you think so. But you forget that you are doing it in order that all these people who don't count may read about it in the papers and so get a little harmless relaxation."

"But we don't do it to get into the papers."

"Probably not. Neither did this—what is it here in my plate, a lamb chop?—this lamb gambol about and keep itself in condition to form a course at Segur's dinner. But after all, wasn't that what it was really for? Then think how many people you support by your work."

"You make me feel like a day-labourer."

"Oh, you're a much harder worker than any day labourer. And the saddest part of it to me is that you work altogether for others. You give, give and get in return nothing but a few flattering glances, a few careless pats on the back of your vanity. I should hate to work so hard for so little."

"But what would you do?" Miss Trevor was looking at him, interested and amused.

"Well, I'd work for myself. I'd insist on a return, on getting back something equivalent or near it. I'd insist on having my mind improved, or having my power or my reputation advanced."

"I was only jesting when I said that about people not counting."

"Altogether?"

"No, not altogether. I don't care much about the masses. They seem to me to be underbred, of a different sort. I hate doing things that are useful and I hate people that do useful things--in a general way, I mean."

"That is doubtless due to defective education," said Howard, with a smile that carried off the thrust as a jest.

"Is that the way you'd describe a horror of contact with—well, with unpleasant things?" Miss Trevor was serious.

"But is it that? Isn't it just an unconscious affectation, taken up simply because all the people about you think that way—if one can call the process thinking? You don't think, do you, that it is a sign of superiority to be narrow, to be ignorant, to be out of touch with the great masses of one's fellow-beings, to play the part of a harlequin or a ballet-girl on the stage of life? I understand how a stupid ass can fritter away his one chance to live in saying and hearing and doing silly things. But ought not an intelligent person try to enjoy life, try to get something substantial out of it, try to possess himself of its ideas and emotions? Why should one play the fool simply because those about one are incapable of playing any other part?"

"I'm surprised that you are here to-night. Still, I suppose you'll give yourself absolution on the plea that one must dine somewhere."

"But I'm not wasting my time. I'm learning. I'm observing a phase of life. And I'm seeing the latest styles in women's gowns and——"

"Is that important—styles, I mean?"

"Do you suppose that my kind of people, the working classes, would spend so much time and thought in making anything that was not important? There is nothing more important."

"Then you don't think we women are wasting time when we talk about dress so much?"

"On the contrary, it is an evidence of your superior sagacity. Women talk trade, 'shop,' as soon as they get away from the men. They talk men and dress—fish and nets."

Berersford heard the word fish and interrupted.

"Do you go South next month, Marian?"

"Yes—about the fifteenth." Miss Trevor explained to Howard: "Bobby—Mr. Berersford here—always fishes in Florida in January."

The conversation again became general and personal. Howard knew none of the people of whom they were talking and all that they said was of the nature of gossip. But they talked in a sparkling way, using good English, speaking in agreeable voices with a correct accent, and indulging in a great deal of malicious humour.

As they separated Mrs. Sidney, to whom Howard had not spoken during the evening, said to Segur: "You must bring Mr. Howard on Sunday afternoon."

"Will you drop Marian at the house for me?" Mrs. Carnarvon asked her. "I want to go on to Edith's."

Segur went with Mrs. Sidney and Marian to their carriage. "Who is Mr. Howard?" Mrs. Sidney said, and Miss Trevor drew nearer to hear the answer.

"One of the editorial writers down on the paper and a very clever one—none better. He works hard and is desperately serious and a regular hermit."

"I think he's very handsome—don't you, Marian?"

"I found him interesting," said Miss Trevor.

Howard thought a great deal about Miss Trevor that night, and she was still in his head the next day. "This comes of never seeing women," he said to himself. "The first girl I meet seems the most beautiful I ever saw, and the most intellectual. And, when I think it over, what did she say that was startling?"

Nevertheless he went with Segur the next Sunday to Mrs. Sidney's great house in the upper Avenue overlooking the Park.

"Why do I come here?" he asked himself. "It is a sheer waste of time. Mrs. Sidney can do me no good, or I her. It must be the hope of seeing Miss Trevor."

When the gaudy and be-powdered flunkey held back the heavy curtains of the salon to announce him and Segur, he saw Miss Trevor on a low chair absently staring into the fire. Yet when he had spoken to Mrs. Sidney and turned toward her she at once stretched out her hand with a slight smile. Some others came in and Howard was free to talk to her. He sat looking at her steadily, admiring her almost perfect profile, delicate yet strong.

"And what have you been doing since I saw you?" Miss Trevor asked.

"Writing little pieces about politics for the paper," replied Howard.

"Politics? I detest it. It is all stealing and calling names, isn't it? And something dreadful is always going to happen if somebody or other isn't elected, or is elected, to something or other. And then, whether he is or not, nothing happens. I should think the men who have been so excited and angry and alarmed would feel very cheap. But they don't. And the next time they carry on in just the same ridiculous way."

"Politics is like everything else—interesting if you understand what it is all about. But like everything else, you can't understand it without a little study at first. It's a pity women don't take an interest. If they did the men might become more reasonable and sane about it than they are now. But you—what have you been doing?"

"I—oh, industriously superintending the making of my new nets." Marian laughed and Howard was flattered. "And also, well, riding in the Park every morning. But I never do anything interesting. I simply drift."

"That's so much simpler and more satisfactory than threshing and splashing about as I do. It seems so fussy and foolish and futile. I wish—that is, sometimes I wish—that I had learned to amuse myself in some less violent and exhausting way."

"Marian—I say, Marian," called Mrs. Sidney. "Has Teddy come down?"

Miss Trevor coloured slightly as she answered: "No, he comes a week Wednesday. He's still hunting."

"Hunting," Howard repeated when Mrs. Sidney was again busy with the others. "Now there is a kind of work that never bothers a man's brains or sets him to worrying. I wish I knew how to amuse myself in some such way."

"You should go about more."

"Go—where?"

"To see people."

"But I do see a great many people. I'm always seeing them—all day long."

"Yes—but that is in a serious way. I mean go where you will be amused—to dinners for instance."

"I don't dare. I can't work at work and also work at play. I must work at one or the other all the time. I can do nothing without a definite object. I can't be just a little interested in anything or anybody. With me it is no interest at all or else absorption until interest is exhausted."

"Then if you were interested in a woman, let us say, you'd be absorbed until you found out all there was, and then you'd—take to your heels."

"But she might always be new. She might interest me more and more. Anyhow I fancy that she would weary of me long before I wearied of her. I think women usually weary first. Men are very monotonous. We are as vain as women, if not vainer, without their capacity for concealing it. And vanity makes one think he does not need to exert himself to please."

"But why do people usually say that it is the men that are difficult to hold?'

"Because the men hold the women, not through the kind of interest we are talking about, but through another kind—quite different. Women are so lazy and so dependent—dependent upon men for homes, for money, for escort even."

Miss Trevor was flushing, as if the fire were too hot—at least she moved a little farther away from it. "Your ideal woman would be a shop-girl, I should say from what you've told me."

"Perhaps—in the abstract. I really do think that if I were going to marry, I should look about for a working-girl, a girl that supported herself. How can a man be certain of the love of a woman who is dependent upon him? I should be afraid she was only tolerating me as a labour-saving device."

Miss Trevor laughed. "There certainly is no vanity in that remark," she said. "Now I can't imagine most of the men I know thinking that."

"It's only theory with me. In practice doubtless I should be as self-complacent as any other man."

They left Mrs. Sidney's together and Howard walked down the Avenue with her. It seemed a wonderful afternoon—the air dazzling, intoxicating. He was filled with the joy of living and was glad this particular tall, slender, distinguished-looking girl was there to make his enjoyment perfect. They were gay with the delight of being young and in health and attractive physically and mentally each to the other. They looked each at the other a great deal, and more and more frankly.

"Am I never to see you again?" he asked as he rang the bell for her.

"I believe Mrs. Carnarvon is going to invite you to dine here Thursday night."

"Thank you," said Howard.

Miss Trevor coloured. But she met his glance boldly and laughed. Howard wondered why her laugh was defiant, almost reckless.

* * * * * * * * *

He saw Segur at the club after dinner that same night. "And how do you like Miss Trevor?" Segur began as the whiskey and carbonic were set before them.

"A very attractive girl," said Howard.

"Yes—so a good many men have thought in the last five years. She's marrying Teddy Danvers in the spring, I believe. At any rate it's generally looked on as settled. Teddy's a good deal of a 'chump.' But he's a decent fellow—good-looking, good-natured, domestic in his tastes, and nothing but money."

Howard was smiling to himself. He understood Miss Trevor's sudden consciousness of the nearness of the fire, her flush when Mrs. Sidney asked about "Teddy," and the recklessness in her parting laugh.

"Well, Teddy's in luck," he said aloud.

"Not so sure of that. She's quite capable of leading him a dance if he bores her. And bore her he will. But that is nothing new. This town is full of it."

"Full of what?"

"Of weary women—weary wives. The men are hobby-riders. They have just one interest and that usually small and dull—stocks or iron or real estate or hunting or automobiles. Our women are not like the English women—stupid, sodden. They are alive, acute. They wish to be interested. Their husbands bore them. So—well, what is the natural temptation to a lazy woman in search of an interest?"

"It's like Paris—like France?"

"Yes, something. Except that perhaps our women are more sentimental, not fond of intrigue for its own sake—at least, not as a rule."

"Doesn't interest them deeply enough, I suppose. It's the American blood coming out—the passion for achievement. They want a man of whom they can be proud, a man who is doing something interesting and doing it well."

"I doubt that," replied Segur shrugging his shoulders. "When a woman loves a man, she wants to absorb him."

Howard soon went away to his rooms for a long evening of undisturbed thought about Teddy Danvers's fiancée—the first temptation that had entered his loneliness since Alice died.

In the few weeks of her illness and the few months immediately following her death, he had been at his very best. He was able to see her as she was and to appreciate her. He was living in the clear pure air of the Valley of the Great Shadow where all things appear in their true relations and true proportions. But only there was it possible for the gap between him and Alice to close—that gap of which she was more acutely conscious than he, and which she made wider far than it really was by being too humble with him, too obviously on her knees before him. Such superiority as she thought he possessed is not in human nature; but neither is it in human nature to refuse worship, to refuse to pose upon a pedestal if the opportunity presses.

In the three years between her death and his meeting Marian, the eternal masculine had been secretly gaining strength to resume its pursuit of the eternal feminine. And the eternal feminine was certainly most alluringly personified in this beautiful, graceful girl, at once appreciative and worthy of appreciation.

Perhaps she appealed most strongly to Howard in her vivid suggestion of the open air—of health and strength and nature. He had been leading a cloistered existence and his blood had grown sluggish. She gave him the sensation that a prisoner gets when he catches a glimpse from his barred window of the fields and the streams radiating the joy of life and freedom. And Marian was of his own kind—like the women among whom he had been brought up. She satisfied his idea of what a "lady" should be, but at the same time she was none the less a woman to him—a woman to love and to be loved; to give him sympathy, companionship; to inspire him to overcome his weaknesses by striving to be worthy of her; to bring into his life that feminine charm without which a man's life must be cold and cheerless.

He knew that he could not marry her, that he had no right to make love to her, that it was unwise to go near her again. But he had no power to resist the temptation. And even in those days he had small regard for the means when the end was one upon which he had fixed his mind. "Why not take what I can get?" he thought, as he dreamed of her. "She's engaged—her future practically settled. Yes, I'll be as happy as she'll let me." And he resumed his idealising.

At his time of life idealisation is still not a difficult or a long process. And in this case there was an ample physical basis for it—and far more of a mental basis than young imagination demands. He took the draught she so frankly offered him ; he added a love potion of his own concocting, and drank it off.

He was in love.

XI.

TRESPASSING.

FOR the first time since he had been in newspaper work, Howard came to the office the next day in a long coat and a top hat. He left early and went for a walk in the Avenue. But Miss Trevor was neither driving nor walking. He repeated this excursion the next afternoon with better success. At Fortieth Street he saw her and her cousin half a block ahead of him. He walked slowly and examined her. She was satisfactory from the aigrette in her hat to her heels—a long, narrow, graceful figure, dressed with the expensive simplicity characteristic of the most intelligent class of the women of New York and Paris. She walked as if she were accustomed to walking. Mrs. Carnarvon had that slight hesitation, almost stumble, which indicates the woman who usually drives and never walks if she can avoid it. As they paused at the crowded crossing of Forty-second Street he joined them. When Mrs. Carnarvon found that he was "just out for the air" she left them, to go home—in Forty-seventh Street, a few doors east of the Avenue.

"Come back to tea with her," she said as she nodded to Howard.

"We have at least an hour." Howard was looking at Miss Trevor with his happiness dancing in his eyes. "Why shouldn't we go to the Park?"

"I believe it's not customary," objected Miss Trevor in a tone that made the walk in the Park a certainty.

"I'm glad to hear that. I don't care to do customary things as a rule."

"I see that you don't."

"Do you say so because I show what I am thinking so plainly that you can't help seeing it—and don't in the least mind?"

"Why shouldn't you be glad to be alive and to be seeing me this fine winter day?"

"Why indeed!" Howard looked at her from head to foot and then into her eyes.

"We are not in the Park yet." Miss Trevor accompanied her hint with a laugh and added: "I feel reckless to-day."

"You mean you forget that there is any to-morrow. *I* have shut out to-morrow ever since I saw you."

"And yesterday?" She noted that he coloured slightly, but continued to look at her, his eyes sad. "But there is a to-morrow," she went on.

"Yes—my work, my career is my to-morrow and yours is——"

"Well?"

"Your engagement, of course."

Miss Trevor flushed, but Howard was smiling and she did not long resist the contagion.

"My to-morrow," he continued, "is far more menacing than yours. Yours is just an ordinary, every-day, cut-and-dried affair. Mine is full of doubts and uncertainties with the chances for failure and disappointment. If I can turn my back on my to-morrow, surely you can waive yours for the moment?"

"But why are you so certain that I wish to?"

"Instinct. I could not be so happy as I am with you if you were not content to have me here."

They spoke little until they were well within the Park. There they turned down a by-path and took the walk skirting the lower lake. Miss Trevor looked at Howard with a puzzled expression.

"I never met any one like you," she said. "I have always felt so sure of myself. You take me off my feet. I feel as if I did not know where I was going and—didn't much care. And that's the worst of it."

"No, the best of it. You are a star going comfortably through your universe in a fixed orbit. You maintain your exact relations with your brother and sister stars. You keep all your engagements, you never wobble in your path—everything exact, mathematical. And up darts a wild-haired, impetuous comet, a hurrying, bustling, irregular wanderer coming from you don't know where, going you don't know whither. We pass very near each to the other. The social astronomers may or may not note a little variation in your movement—a very little, and soon over. They probably will not note the insignificant meteor that darted close up to you—close enough to get his poor face sadly scorched and his long hair cruelly singed—and then hurried sadly away. And——"

"And—what? Isn't there any more to the story?" Marian's eyes were shining with a light which she was conscious had never been there before.

"And—and——" Howard stopped and faced her. His hands were thrust deep in the pockets of his overcoat. He looked at her in a way that made the colour fly from her face and then leap back again. "And—I love you."

"Oh"—Marian said, hiding her face in her white muff. "Oh."

"I don't wish to touch you," he went on, "I just wish to look at you—so tall, so straight, so—so alive, and to love you and be happy." Then he laughed and turned. "But you'll catch cold. Let us walk on."

"So you are trying to make a career?" she asked after a few minutes' silence.

"Yes—trying—or, rather, I was. And shall again when you have gone your way and I mine."

Marian was amazed at herself. Every tradition, every instinct of her life was being trampled by this unknown whom she had just met. And she was assisting in the trampling. In fact it was difficult for her to restrain herself from leading in the iconoclasm. She looked at him in wonder and delighted terror.

"Why do you look at me in that way?" he said, turning his head suddenly.

"Because you are stronger than I—and I am afraid—yet I—well—I like it."

"It is not I that is stronger than you, nor you that are stronger than I. It is a third that is stronger than both of us. I need not mention the gentleman's name?"

"It is not necessary. But I'd like to hear you pronounce it. At least I did a moment ago."

"I'll not risk repetition. I've been thinking of what might have been."

"What?" Marian laughed a little, rather satirically. "A commonplace engagement and a commonplace wedding and a commonplace honeymoon leading into a land of commonplace disillusion and yawning—or worse?"

"Not unlikely. But since we're only dreaming

why not dream more to our taste? Now as I look at your strong, clear, ambitious profile, I can dream of a career made by two working as one, working cheerfully day in and day out, fair and foul weather, working with the certainty of success as the crown."

"But failure might come."

"It couldn't. We wouldn't work for fame or for riches or for any outside thing. We would work to make ourselves wiser and better and more worthy each of the other and both of our great love."

Again they were walking in silence.

"I am so sad," Marian said at last. "But I am so happy too. What has come over me? But—you will work on, won't you? And you will accomplish everything. Yes, I am sure you will."

"Oh, I'll work—in my own way. And I'll get a good deal of what I want. But not everything. You say you can't understand yourself. No more can I understand myself. I thought my purpose fixed. I knew that I had nothing to do with marrying and giving in marriage, so I kept away from danger. And here, as miraculously as if a thunderbolt had dropped from this open winter sky, here is—you."

They were in the Avenue again—"the awakening," Howard said as the flood of carriages rolled about them.

"You will win," she repeated, when they were

almost at Forty-seventh Street. "You will be famous."

"Probably not. The price for fame may be too big."

"The price? But you are willing to work?"

"Work—yes. But not to lie, not to cheat, not to exchange self-respect for self-contempt—at least, I think, I hope not."

"But why should that be necessary?"

"It may not be if I am free—free to meet every situation as it arises, with no responsibility for others resting upon me in the decision. If I had a wife, how could I be free? I might be forced to sell myself—not for fame but for a bare living. Suppose choice between freedom with poverty and comfort with self-contempt were put squarely at me, and I a married man. She would decide, wouldn't she?"

"Yes, and if she were the right sort of a woman, decide instantly for self-respect."

"Of course—if I asked her. But do you imagine that when a man loves a woman he lets her know?"

"It would be a crime not to let her know."

"It would be a greater crime to put her to the test—if she were a woman brought up, say, as you have been."

"How can you say that? How can you so over-estimate the value of mere incidentals?"

"How can I? Because I have known poverty—have known what it was to look want in the face. Because I have seen women, brought up as you have been, crawling miserably about in the sloughs of poverty. Because I have seen the weaknesses of human nature and know that they exist in me—yes, and in you, for all your standing there so strong and arrogant and self-reliant. It is easy to talk of misery when one does not understand it. It is easy to be the martyr of an hour or a day. But to drag into a sordid and squalid martyrdom the woman one loves—well, the man does not live who would do it, if he knew what I know, had seen what I have seen. No, love is a luxury of the rich and the poor and the steady-going. It is not for my kind, not for me."

They were pausing at Mrs. Carnarvon's door.

"I shall not come in this afternoon," he said. "But to-morrow—if I don't come in to-day, don't you think it will be all right for me to come then?"

"I shall expect you," she said.

The talk of those who had come in for tea seemed artificial and flat. She soon went up-stairs, eager to be alone. Mechanically she went to her desk to write her customary daily letter to Danvers. She looked vacantly at the pen and paper, and then she remembered why she was sitting there.

"You are a traitor," she said to her reflection in the mirror over the desk. "But you will pay for your treason. Has not one a right to that for which she is willing to pay?"

XII.

MAKING THE MOST OF A MONTH.

To be sure of a woman a man must be confident either of his own powers or of her absolute frankness and honesty. It was self-assurance that made Edward Danvers blindly confident of Marian.

His father, a man with none but selfish uses for his fellow men, had given him a pains-taking training as a vigilant guard for a great fortune. His favourite maxim was, "Always look for motives." And he once summed up his own character and idea of life by saying: "I often wake at night and laugh as I think how many men are lying awake in their beds, scheming to get something out of me for nothing."

There could be but one result of such an education by such an educator. Danvers was acutely suspicious, saved from cynicism and misanthropy by his vanity only. He was the familiar combination of credulity and incredulity, now trusting not at all and again trusting with an utter incapacity to judge. Had he been far more attractive personally, he might still have failed to find genuine affection. To be liked for one's self alone or even chiefly is rarely the lot of any human being who has a possession that is all but universally coveted—wealth or position or power or beauty.

Danvers and Marian had known each the other from childhood. And she perhaps came nearer to liking him for himself than did any one else of his acquaintance. She was used to his conceit, his selfishness, his meanness and smallness in suspicion, his arrogance, his narrow-mindedness. She knew his good qualities —his kindness of heart, his shamed-face generosity, his honesty, the strong if limited sense of justice which made him a good employer and a good landlord. They had much in common—the same companions, the same idea of the agreeable and the proper, the same passion for out-door life, especially for hunting. He fell in love with her when she came back from two years in England and France, and she thought that she was in love with him. She undoubtedly was fond of him, proud of his handsome, athletic look and bearing, proud of his skill and daring in the hunting field.

One day—it was in the autumn a year before Howard met her—they were "in at the death" together after a run across a stiff country that included several dangerous jumps. "You're the only one that can keep up with me," he said, admiring her glowing face and star-like eyes, her graceful, assured seat on a hunter that no one else either cared or dared to ride.

"You mean you are the only one who can keep up with *me*," she laughed, preparing for what his face warned her was coming.

"No I don't, Marian dear. I mean that we ought to go right on keeping up with each other. You won't say no, will you?"

Marian was liking him that day—he was looking his best. She particularly liked his expression as he proposed to her. She had intended to pretend to refuse him; instead her colour rose and she said: "No—which means yes. Everybody expects it of us, Teddy. So I suppose we mustn't disappoint them."

The fact that "everybody" did expect it, the fact that he was the great "catch" in their set, with his two hundred and fifty thousand a year, his good looks and his good character—these were her real reasons, with the first dominant. But she did not admit it to herself then. At twenty-four even the mercenary instinct tricks itself out in a most deceptive romantic disguise if there is the ghost of an opportunity. Besides, there was no reason, and no sign of an approaching reason, for the shadow of a suspicion that life with Teddy Danvers would not be full of all that she and her friends regarded as happiness.

But she would not marry immediately. She was tenacious of her freedom. She was restless, dissatisfied with herself and not elated by her prospects. She had an excellent mind, reasonable, appreciative, ambitious. Until she "came out" she had spent much time among books; but as she had had no capable director of her reading, she got from it only a vague sense that there was somewhere something in the way of achievement which she might possibly like to attain if she knew what it was or where to look for it. As she became settled in her place in the routine of social life, as her horizon narrowed to the conventional ideas of her set, this sense of possible and attractive achievement became vaguer. But her restlessness did not diminish.

"I never saw such an ungrateful girl," was Mrs. Carnarvon's comment upon one of Marian's outbursts of almost peevish fretting. "What do you want?"

"That's just it," exclaimed Marian, half-laughing. "What *do* I want? I look all about me and I can't see it. Yet I know that there must be something. I think I ought to have been a man. Sometimes I feel like running away—away off somewhere. I feel as if I were getting second-bests, paste substitutes for the real jewels. I feel as I did when I was a child and demanded the moon. They gave me a little gilt crescent and said: 'Here is a nice little moon for baby;' and it made me furious."

Mrs. Carnarvon looked irritated. "I don't understand it. You are getting the best of everything. Of course you can't expect to be happy. I don't suppose that any one is happy. But all the solid things of life are yours, and you can and should be comfortable and contented."

"That's just it," answered Marian indignantly. "I have always been swaddled in cotton wool. I have never been allowed really to feel. I think it is the spirit of revolt in me. Yes, I ought to have been a man. I'm sure that then I could have made life a little less tiresome."

It was this dissatisfaction that postponed the announcement of the engagement from month to month until a year had slipped away.

Instead of coming to New York, Danvers went off to Montana for a mountain-lion hunt with two Englishmen who had been staying with him in "The Valley." He would join Marian for the trip South, the engagement would be announced, and the wedding would be in May—such was the arrangement which Marian succeeded in making. It settled everything and at the same time it gave her a month of freedom in New York. She hinted enough of this programme to Howard to enable him to grasp its essential points.

"A month's holiday," was his comment. They were alone on the second seat of George Browning's coach, driving through the Park. "If we were like those people"—he was looking at a young man and young woman, side by side upon a Park bench, blue with cold but absorbed in themselves and obviously ecstatic. Marian glanced at them with slightly supercilious amusement and became so interested that she turned her head to follow them with her eyes after the coach had passed.

"Is he kissing her?" asked Howard.

"No—not yet. But I'm sure he will as soon as we have turned the corner." She said nothing for a moment or two, her glance straight ahead and upon vacancy, he admiring the curve of her cheek at the edge of its effective framing of fur.

"But we are not——" She spoke in a low tone, regretful, pensive, almost sad. "We are not like them."

"Oh, yes we are. But—we fancy we are not. We've sold our birthright, our freedom, our independence for—for——"

"Well—what?"

"Baubles— childish toys— vanities — s h a d o w s. Doesn't it show what ridiculous little creatures we human beings are that we regard the most valueless things as of the highest value, and think least of the true valuables. For, tell me, Lady-Whom-I-Love, what is most valuable in the few minutes of this little journey among the stars on the good ship Mother Earth?"

"But you would not care always as you care now? It would not, could not, last. If we—if we were like those people on the bench back there, we'd go on and—and spoil it all."

"Perhaps—who can say? But in some circumstances couldn't I make you just as happy as—as some one else could?"

"Not if you had made me infinitely happier at one time than even you could hope to make me all the time. At least I think not. It would always be—be racing against a record; we both would be, wouldn't we?"

Howard looked at her with an expression which transfigured his face and sent the colour flaming to her cheeks. "That being the case," he said, "let us—let us make the record one that will not be forgotten—soon."

During the month he saw her almost every day. She was most ingenious in arranging these meetings. They were together afternoons and evenings. They were often alone. Yet she was careful not to violate any convention, always to keep, or seem to be keeping, one foot "on the line." Howard threw himself into his infatuation with all his power of concentration He practically took a month's holiday from the office. He thought about her incessantly. He used all his skill with words in making love to her. And she abandoned herself to an equal infatuation with equal absorption. Neither of them spoke of the past or the future. They lived in the present, talked of the present.

One day she spoke of herself as an orphan.

"I did not know that," he said. "But then what do I know about you in relation to the rest of the world? To me you are an isolated act of creation."

"You must tell me about *your*self." She was looking at him, surprised. "Why, I know nothing at all about you."

"Oh, yes, you do. You know all that there is to know—all that is important."

"What?" She was asking for the pleasure of hearing him say it.

"That I love you—you—all of you—all of you, with all of me."

Her eyes answered for her lips, which only said smilingly: "No, we haven't time to get acquainted—at least not to-day."

* * * * * * * * *

She was to start for Florida at ten the next morning. Mrs. Carnarvon was going away to the opera, giving them the last evening alone. Marian had asked this of her point-blank.

"You are an extraordinarily sensible as well as strong-willed girl, Marian," Mrs. Carnarvon replied.

"I can't find it in my heart to blame you for what you're doing. The fact that I haven't even hinted a protest, but have lent myself to your little plots, shows that that young man has hypnotized me also."

"You needn't disturb yourself, as you know," Marian said gaily. "I'm not hypnotized. I shall not see Mr. Howard again until—after it's all over. Perhaps not then."

He came to dinner and they were not alone until almost nine. She sat near the open fire among the cushions heaped high upon the little sofa. She had never been more beautiful, and apparently never in a happier mood. They both laughed and talked as if it were the first instead of the last day of their month. Neither spoke of the parting; each avoided all subjects that pointed in direction of the one subject of which both thought whenever their minds left the immediate present. As the little clock on the mantle began to intimate in a faint, polite voice the quarter before eleven, he said abruptly, almost brusquely:

"I feel like a coward, giving you up in this way. Yes—giving you up; for you have a traitor in your fortress who has offered me the keys, who offers them to me now. But I do not trust you; and I can't trust myself. The curse of luxury is on you, the curse of ambition on me. If we had found each the other younger; if I had lived less alone, more in the ordinary habit of dependence upon others; if you had been brought up to live instead of to have all the machinery of living provided and conducted for you —well, it might have been different."

"You are wrong as to me, right as to yourself. But yours is not the curse of ambition. It is the passion for freedom. It would be madness for you, thinking as you do, even if you could—and you can't."

He stood up and held out his hand. She did not rise or look at him.

"Good night," she said at last, putting her hand in his. "Of course I am thinking I shall see you to-morrow. One does not come out of such a dream," —she looked up at him smiling—"all in a moment."

"Good night," he smiled back at her. "I shall not open 'the fiddler's bill' until—until I have to." At the door he turned. She had risen and was kneeling on the sofa, her elbow on its low arm, her chin upon her hand, her eyes staring into the fire. He came toward her.

"May I kiss you?" he said.

"Yes." Her voice was expressionless.

He bent over and just touched his lips to the back of her neck at the edge of her hair. He thought that she trembled slightly, but her face was set and she did not look toward him. He turned and left her. Half an hour later she heard the bell ring—it was Mrs. Carnarvon. She wished to see no one, so she fled through the rear door of the reception room and up the great stairway to lock herself in her boudoir. She sank slowly upon the lounge in front of the fire and closed her eyes. The fire died out and the room grew cold. A warning chilliness made her rise to get ready for bed.

"No," she said aloud. "It isn't ambition and it isn't lack of love. It's a queer sort of cowardice; but it's cowardice for all that. He's a coward or he wouldn't have given up. But—I wonder—how am I going to live without him? I need him—more than he needs me, I'm afraid."

She was standing before her dressing table. On it was a picture of Danvers—handsome, self-satisfied, healthy, unintellectual. She looked at it, gave a little shiver, and with the end of her comb toppled it over upon its face.

XIII.

RECKONING WITH DANVERS.

ON that journey south Marian for the first time studied Danvers as a husband in prospect.

The morning after they left New York, their private car arrived at Savannah. At dark the night before they were rushing through a snow storm raging in a wintry landscape. Now they were looking out upon spring from the open windows. As soon as the train stopped, all except Marian and Danvers left the car to walk up and down the platform. Danvers, standing behind Marian, looked around to make sure that none of the servants was about, then rubbed his hand caressingly and familiarly upon her cheek.

"Did you miss me?" he asked.

Marian could not prevent her head from shrinking from his touch.

"There's nobody about," Danvers said, reassuringly. But he acted upon the hint and, taking his hand away, came around and sat beside her.

"Did you miss me?" he repeated, looking at her with an expression in his frank, manly blue eyes that made her flush at the thought of "treason" past and to come.

"Did *you* miss *me*?" she evaded.

"I would have returned long ago if I had not been ashamed," he answered, smiling. "I never thought that I should come not to care for as good shooting as that. You almost cost me my life."

"Yes?" Marian spoke absently. She was absorbed in her mental comparison of the two men.

"I got away from the others and was looking at your picture. They started up a lion and he came straight at me from behind. If he hadn't made a misstep in his hurry and loosened a stone, I guess he would have got me. As it was, I got him."

"You mean your gun got him."

"Of course. You don't suppose I tackled him bare-handed."

"It might have been fairer. I don't see how you can boast of having killed a creature that never bothered you, that you had to go thousands of miles out of your way to find, and that you attacked with a gun, giving him no chance to escape."

"What nonsense!" laughed Danvers. "I never expected to hear you say anything like that. Who's been putting such stuff into your head?"

Marian coloured. She did not like his tone. She resented the suggestion of the truth that her speech was borrowed. It made her uncomfortable to find herself thus unexpectedly on the dangerous ground.

"I suppose it must have been that newspaper fellow Mrs. Carnarvon has taken up. She talked about him for an hour after you left us to go to bed last night."

"Yes, it was—was Mr. Howard." Marian had recovered herself. "I want you to meet him some time. You'll like him, I'm sure."

"I doubt it. Mrs. Carnarvon seemed not to know much about him. I suppose he's more or less of an adventurer."

Marian wondered if this obvious dislike was the result of one of those strange instincts that sometimes enable men to scent danger before any sign of it appears.

"Perhaps he is an adventurer," she replied. "I'm sure I don't know. Why should one bother to find out about a passing acquaintance? It is enough to know that he is amusing."

"I'm not so sure of that. He might make off with the jewels when you had your back turned."

As soon as she had made her jesting denial of her real lover Marian was ashamed of herself. And Danvers' remark, though a jest, cut her. "What I said about a passing acquaintance was not just or true," she said impulsively and too warmly. "Mr. Howard is not an adventurer. I admire and like him very much indeed. I'm proud of his friendship."

Danvers shrugged his shoulders and looked at her suspiciously.

"You saw a good deal of this—this friend of yours?" he demanded, his mouth straightening into a dictatorial line.

At this Marian grew haughty and her eyes flashed: "Why do you ask?" she inquired, her tone dangerously calm.

"Because I have the right to know." He pointed to the diamond on her third finger.

"Oh—that is soon settled." Marian drew off the ring and held it out to him. "Really, Teddy, I think you ought to have waited a little longer before insisting so fiercely on your rights."

"Don't be absurd, Marian." Danvers did not take the ring but fixed his eyes upon her face and changed his tone to friendly remonstrance. "You know the ring doesn't mean anything. It's your promise that counts. And honestly don't you think your promise does give me the right to ask you about your new friends when you speak of them, of one of them, in—in such a way?"

"I don't intend to deceive you," she said, turning the ring around slowly on her finger. "I didn't know how to tell you. I suppose the only way to speak is just to speak."

"Do you think you are in love with this man, Marian?"

She nodded, then after a long pause, said, "Yes, Teddy, I love him."

"But I thought——"

"And so did I, Teddy. But he came, and I—well I couldn't help it."

As he did not speak, she looked at him. His face was haggard and white and in his eyes which met hers frankly there was suffering.

"It wasn't my fault, Teddy," Marian laid her hand on his arm, "at least, not altogether. I might have kept away and I didn't."

"Oh, I don't blame you. I blame him."

"But it wasn't his fault. I—I—encouraged him."

"Did he know that we were engaged?"

"Yes," reluctantly.

"The scoundrel! I suspected that he was rotten somewhere."

"You are unjust to him. I have not told you properly."

"Did he tell you that he cared for you?"

"Yes—but he didn't try to get me to break my engagement."

"So much the more a scoundrel, he. Tell me,

Marian—come to your senses and tell me—what in the devil did he hang about you for and make love to you, if he didn't want to marry you? Would an honest man, a decent man, do that?"

Marian's face confessed assent.

"I should think you would have seen what sort of a fellow he is. I should think you would despise him."

"Sometimes it seems to me that I ought to. But I always end by despising myself—and—and—it makes no difference in the way I feel toward him."

"I think I would do well to look him up and give him a horse-whipping. But you'll get over him, Marian. I am astonished at your cousin. How could she let this go on? But then, she's crazy about him too."

Marian smiled miserably. "I've owned up and you ought to congratulate yourself on so luckily getting rid of such an untrustworthy person as I."

"Getting rid of you?" Danvers looked at her defiantly. "Do you think I'm going to let you go on and ruin yourself on an impulse? Not much! I hold you to your promise. You'll come round all right after you've been away from this fellow for a few days. You'll be amazed at yourself a week from now."

"You don't understand, Teddy." Marian wished

him to see once for all that, whatever might be the future for her and Howard, there was no future for her and him. "Don't make it so hard for me to tell you."

"I don't want to hear any more about it now, Marian. I can't stand it—I hardly know what I'm saying—wait a few days—let's go on as we have been—here they come."

The others of the party came bustling into the car and the train started. For the rest of the journey Danvers avoided her, keeping to the smoking room and the game of poker there. Marian could neither read nor watch the landscape. She did not know whether to be glad or sorry that she had told him. She hated to think that she had inflicted pain and she could not believe, in spite of what she had seen in his eyes, that his feeling in the matter was more than jealousy and wounded vanity.

"He doesn't really care for me," she thought. "It's his pride that is hurt. He will flare out at me and break it off. I do hope he'll get angry. It will make it so much easier for me."

Late in the afternoon she took Mrs. Carnarvon into her confidence. "I've told Teddy," she said.

"I might have known!" exclaimed her cousin. "What on earth made you do that?"

"I don't know—perhaps shame."

"Shame—trash! Your life is going to be a fine turmoil if you run to Teddy with an account of every little mild flirtation you happen to have. Of all the imbeciles, the most imbecile is the woman who confesses."

"But how could I marry him when——"

"When you don't love him?"

"No—I might have done that. I like him. But, when I love another man."

"It does make a difference. But you ought to be able to foresee that you'll get over Howard in a few weeks——"

"Precisely what Teddy said."

"Did he? I'm surprised at his having so much sense. For, if you'll forgive me, I don't think Teddy will ever set New York on fire—at least, he's—well, he has the makings of an ideal husband. And has he broken it off?"

"No. He wouldn't have it."

"Really? Well he *is* in love. Most men in his position—able to get any girl he wants—would have thrown up the whole business. Yes, he must be awfully in love."

"Do you think that?" Marian's voice spoke distress but she felt only satisfaction. "Oh, I hope not—that is, I'd like to think he cared a great deal and at the same time I don't want to hurt him."

"Don't fret yourself about these two men. Just go on thinking as you please. You'll be surprised how soon Howard will fade." Mrs. Carnarvon smiled satirically at some thought—perhaps a memory. "You're a good deal of a goose, my dear, but you are a great deal more of a woman. That's why I feel sure that Teddy will win."

With such an opportunity—with the field clear and the woman half-remorseful over her treachery, half-indignant at the man who had shown himself so weak and spiritless—a cleverer or a less vain man than Danvers would have triumphed easily. And for the first week he did make progress. He acted upon the theory that Marian had been hypnotized and that the proper treatment was to ignore her delusion and to treat her with assiduous but not annoying consideration. He did not pose as an injured or jealous lover. He was the friend, always at her service, always thinking out plans for her amusement. He made no reference to their engagement or to Howard.

Several people of their set were at the hotel and Marian was soon drifting back into her accustomed modes of thought. The wider horizon which she fancied Howard had shown her was growing dim and hazy. The horizon which he had made her think narrow was beginning again to seem the only one.

This meant Danvers; but he was not acute enough to understand her and to follow up his advantage.

One morning as he was walking up and down under the palms, waiting for Mrs. Carnarvon and Marian, Mrs. Fortescue called him. She was a cold, rather handsome woman. In her eyes was the expression that always betrays the wife or the mistress who loathes the man she lives with, enduring him only because he gives her that which she most wants—money. She had one fixed idea—to marry her daughter "well," that is, to money.

"Can you join us to-day, Teddy?" she asked. "We need one more man."

"I'm waiting for Mrs. Carnarvon and Marian," he explained.

"Oh, of course." Mrs. Fortescue smiled. "What a nice girl she is—so clever, so—so independent. I admired her immensely for deciding to marry that poor, obscure young fellow. I like to see the young people romantic."

Danvers flushed angrily and pulled at his mustache. He tried to smile. "We've teased her about it a good deal," he said, "but she denies it."

"I suppose they aren't ready to announce the engagement yet," Mrs. Fortescue suggested. "I suppose they are waiting until he betters his position a little. It's never a good idea to have too long a time between the announcement and the marriage."

"Perhaps that is it." Danvers tried to look indifferent but his eyes were sullen with jealousy.

"I always rather thought that you and Marian were going to make a match of it," continued Mrs. Fortescue. Just then her daughter came down the walk. She was fashionably dressed in white and blue that brought out all the loveliness of her golden hair and violet eyes and faintly-coloured, smooth fair skin. Danvers had not seen her since she "came out," and was dazzled by her radiance.

They say that every man must be a little in love with every pretty woman he sees. And Danvers at once gave Ellen Fortescue her due. She sat silent beside her mother, looking the personification of innocence, purity and poetry. Her mother continued subtly to poison Danvers against Marian, to make him feel that she had not appreciated him, that she had trifled with him, that she had not treated him as his dignity and importance merited. When she and Mrs. Carnarvon appeared, he joined them tardily, after having made an arrangement with the Fortescues for the next day.

That evening he danced several times with Ellen Fortescue and adopted the familiar lover's tactics—he set about making Marian jealous. He scored the customary success. When she went to bed she lay for several hours looking out into the moonlight, raging against the Fortescues and against Danvers. The mere fact that a man whom she regarded as hers was permitting himself to show marked attention to another woman would have been sufficient. But in addition, Marian was perfectly aware of the material advantages of this particular man. She did not want to marry him; at least she was of that mind at the moment. But she might change her mind. Certainly, if there was to be any breaking off, she wished it to be of her doing. She did not fancy the idea of him departing joyfully.

She was far too wise to show that she saw what was going on. She praised Miss Fortescue to Danvers with apparent frankness and insisted on him devoting more time to her. Danvers persisted in his scheme boldly for a week and then, just as Marian was despairing and was casting about for another plan of campaign, he gave in. They were sitting apart in the shadow near one of the windows of the ball-room. He had been sullen all the evening, almost rude.

"How much longer are you going to keep me in suspense?" he burst out angrily.

"In suspense?"

"You know what I mean. I think I've been very patient."

"You mean our engagement?" Marian was looking at him, repelled by his expression, his manner, the tone of his voice, his whole mood.

"Yes—I want your decision."

"I have not changed."

"You still love that—that newspaper fellow?"

"No, I don't mean that." Marian felt her irritation against Danvers suddenly vanish and in its place a sense of relief and of calmness. "I mean toward you. It won't do, Teddy. We shall get on well as friends. But I can't think of you in—in that way."

Mrs. Fortescue had so swollen his vanity that he was astounded at Marian's decision. He rapidly went over in his mind all the advantages he offered as a husband, and then looked at her as if he thought her beside herself.

"Look here, Marian," he protested. "You can't mean it. Why, it's all settled that we are to marry. It would be madness for you to break it off. I can give you everything—everything. And he can't give you anything." Then with fatal tactlessness: "He won't even give you the little that he can, according to your own story."

"Yes, it's madness, isn't it, Teddy, to refuse you—fascinating you, who can give everything. But that's just it. You have too much. You overwhelm me.

I should feel like a cheat, taking so much and giving so little."

"Don't," he begged, his self-complacence and superiority all gone. "Don't mind my blundering, please, dear. I want you. I can't say it. I haven't any gift of words. But you've known me all my life and you know that I love you. I've set my heart on it, Mary Ann,"—it was the name he used to tease her with when they were children playing together—"You won't go back on me now, will you?"

"I wish I could do as you wish, Teddy." Marian was forgetful of everything but the unhappiness she was causing this friend of so many, many years and of so many, many memories. "But I can't—I can't."

"Marry me, dear, anyhow. You will care afterward." Marian was silent and Danvers hoped. "You know all about me. I'll not give you any surprises. I shan't bother you. And I'll make you happy."

"No," she said firmly. "You mustn't ask it. I'll tell you why. I have thought of marrying you regardless of this. Only last night I thought of it—finally, went over the whole thing. Listen, Teddy—if I were married to you—and if he should come—and he would come sooner or later—if he should come and say 'Come with me,'—I'd go—yes, I'm sure I'd go. I can't explain why. But I know that nothing would stand in the way—nothing."

"You ought to be ashamed of yourself." Marian shrank from him. She was horrified by the malignant fury that sparkled in his eyes and raged in his voice. "That damned scoundrel is worthy of you and you of him. But I'll get you yet. I never was crossed in anything in my life and I'll not be beaten here."

"And I thought you were my friend!" Marian was looking at him, pale, her eyes wide with amazement. "Is it really you?"

He laughed insolently. "Yes—you'll see. And he'll see. I'll crush him as if he were an egg shell. And as for you—you perjurer—you liar!"

He looked at her with coarse contempt, rose and stalked away. Marian sat rigid. She was conscious of the insult. But even that humiliation was not so strong in her mind as the astounding revelation of Danvers. She remembered that even as his eyes blazed hatred at her, he looked at her, at her neck, her bare arms, with the baffled desire of brute passion. She did not fully understand the look, but she felt that it was a degradation far greater than his insulting words.

She slipped, almost skulked to her room, her eyes down, her face in a burning flush, her scarf drawn tightly about her neck. As her door closed behind her, she fell upon her bed and began to sob hysterically. She started up with a scream to find her cousin standing beside her.

"I'm so sorry. Forgive me." Mrs. Carnarvon's voice had lost its wonted levity. "I saw that you were in trouble and followed. I knocked and I thought I heard you answer. What is it, Marie? May I ask? Can I do anything?"

Marian drew her down to the bed and buried her face in her lap. "Oh, I feel so unclean," she said. "It was—Teddy. Would you believe it, Jessie, Teddy! I looked on him as a brother. And he showed me that he was not my friend—that he didn't even love me—that he—oh, I shall never forget the look in his eyes. He made me feel like a—like a *thing*."

Mrs. Carnarvon smothered a smile. "Of course Teddy's a brute," she said. "I thought you knew. He's a domesticated brute, like most of the men and some of the women. You'll have to get used to that."

By refusing to fall in with her mood, Mrs. Carnarvon had gone far toward curing it. Marian stopped sobbing and presently said:

"Oh, I know all that. But I didn't expect it from Teddy—and toward me. And—" she shuddered—"I was thinking, actually thinking of marrying him. I wish never to see him again. And he pretended to be my friend!"

"And he was, no doubt, until he got you on the

brain in another way, in the way he calls love. There isn't any love that has friendship in it."

"We must go away at once."

"Unless Teddy saves us the trouble by going first, as I suspect he will."

"Jessie, he hates me and—and—Mr. Howard."

"So you talked to him about Howard again, did you?" Mrs. Carnarvon was indignant. "You are old enough to know better, Marian. You carry frankness entirely too far. There is such a thing as truth running amuck."

"He said he would crush Howard. And I believe he really meant it."

"Teddy is a man who believes in revenges—or thinks he does. His father taught him to keep accounts in grievances, and no doubt he has opened an account with Howard. But don't be disturbed about it. His father would have insisted on balancing the account. Teddy will just keep on hating, but won't do anything. He's not underhanded."

"He's everything that is vile and low."

"You're quite mistaken, my dear. He's what they call a manly fellow—a little too masculine perhaps, but——"

A knock interrupted and Mrs. Carnarvon, answering it, took from the bell-boy a note for Marian who read it, then handed it to her. Mrs. Carnarvon read:

"I apologise for the way I said what I did this evening, not for what I said. Because you had forgotten yourself, had played the traitor and the cheat was, perhaps, no excuse for my rudeness. You have fallen under an evil influence. I hope no harm will come to you, for I can't get over my feeling for you. But I have done my best and have not been able to save you. I am going away early in the morning.

"E. D."

"Melodramatic, isn't it?" laughed Mrs. Carnarvon. "So he's off. How furious Martha Fortescue and Ellen will be. But they'll go in pursuit, and they'll get him. A man is never so susceptible as when he's broken-hearted. Well, I must go. Good-night, dear. Don't mope and whine. Take your punishment sensibly. You've learned something—if it's only not to tell one man how much you love another."

"I think I'll go abroad with Aunt Retta next month."

"A good idea—you'll forget both these men. Good-night."

"Good-night," answered Marian dolefully, expecting to resume her thoughts of Danvers. But, instead, he straightway disappeared from her mind and she could think only of Howard. She was free now. The one barrier between him and her of which she had been really conscious was gone. And her heart began to ache with longing for him. Why had he not written? What was he doing? Did he really love her or was his passion for her only a flash of a strong and swift imagination?

No, he loved her—she could not doubt that. But she could not understand his conduct. She felt that she ought to be very unhappy, yet she was not. The longer she thought of him and the more she weighed his words and looks, the stronger became her trust in him. "He loves me," she said. "He will come when he can. It may be even harder for him than for me."

And so, explanation failing—for she rejected every explanation that reflected upon him—she hid and excused him behind that familiar refuge of the doubting, mystery.

XIV.

THE NEWS-RECORD GETS A NEW EDITOR.

A FEW minutes after leaving Marian that last night at Mrs. Carnarvon's, Howard was deep in a mood of self-contempt. He felt that he had faced the crisis like a coward. He despised the weakness which enfeebled him for effort to win her and at the same time made it impossible for him to thrust her from his mind.

In the working hours his will conquered with the aid of fixed habit and he was able to concentrate upon his editorials. But in his rooms, and especially after the lights were out, his imagination became master, deprived him of sleep and occasionally lifted him to a height of hope in order that it might dash him down the more cruelly upon the rocks of fact.

At last he was forced to face the situation—in his own evasive fashion. It was impossible to go back. That loneliness which often threatened him after Alice's death had become the permanent condition of his life. " I will work for her," he said. " Until I have made a place for her I dare not claim her. So much I will concede to my weakness. But when I have won a position which reasonably assures the future, I shall claim her—no matter what has happened in the meanwhile."

He would have smiled at this wild resolution had he been in a less distracted state of mind or had he been dealing with any other than a matter of love. But in the circumstances it gave him heart and set him to work with an energy and effectiveness which still further increased Mr. Malcolm's esteem for him.

"Will you dine with me at the Union Club on Wednesday?" Mr. Malcolm asked one morning in mid-February. "Mr. Coulter and Mr. Stokely are coming. I want you to know them better."

Howard accepted and wondered that he took so little interest. For Stokely and Coulter were the principal stockholders of the *News-Record*, and with Malcolm formed the triumvirate which directed it in all its departments. Mr. Malcolm held only a few shares of stock, but received what was in the newspaper-world an immense salary—thirty thousand a year. He was at once an able editor and an able diplomatist. He knew how to make the plans of his two associates conform to conditions of news and policy—when to let them use the paper, or, rather, when to use the paper himself for their personal interests; when and how to induce them to let the paper alone. Through a quarter of a century of changing ownerships Malcolm had persisted, chiefly because he had but one conviction—that the post of editor of the *News-Record* exactly suited him and must remain his at any sacrifice of personal character.

Howard had met Stokely and Coulter. He liked Stokely who was owner of a few shares more than one-third; he disliked Coulter who owned just under one-half.

Stokely was a frank, coarse, dollar-hunter, cheerfully unscrupulous in a large way, acute, caring not at all for principles of any kind, letting the paper alone most of the time because he was astute enough to know that in his ignorance of journalism he would surely injure it as a property.

Coulter was a hypocrite and a snob. Also he fancied he knew how to conduct a newspaper. He was as unscrupulous as Stokely but tried to mask it.

When Stokely wished the *News-Record* to advocate a "job," or steal, or the election of some disreputable who would work in his interest, he told Malcolm precisely what he wanted and left the details of the stultification to his experienced adroitness. When Coulter wished to "poison the fountain of publicity," as Malcolm called the paper's departures from honesty and right, he approached the subject by stealth, trying to convince Malcolm that the wrong was not really wrong, but was right unfortunately disguised.

He would take Malcolm into his confidence by slow and roundabout steps, thus multiplying his difficulties in discharging his "duty." If Coulter's son had not been married to Malcolm's daughter, it is probable that not even his complete subserviency would have enabled him to keep his place.

"If you had told me frankly what you wanted in the first place, Mr. Coulter," he said after an exasperating episode in which Coulter's Pharisaic sensitiveness had resulted in Malcolm's having to "flop" the paper both editorially and in its news columns twice in three days, "we would not have made ourselves ridiculous and contemptible. The public is an ass, but it is an ass with a memory at least three days long. Your stealthiness has made the ass bray at us instead of with and for us. And that is dangerous when you consider that running a newspaper is like running a restaurant—you must please your customers every day afresh."

Coulter was further difficult because of his anxieties about social position for himself and his family. He was disturbed whenever the *News-Record* published an item that might offend any of the people whose acquaintance he had gained with so much difficulty, and for whose good will he was willing to sacrifice even considerable money. Personally, but very privately, he edited the *News-Record's* "fashionable intelligence" columns on Sunday and made them an exhibit of his own sycophancy and snobbishness which excited the amused disgust of all who were in the secret.

Malcolm liked Howard, admired him, in a way envied his fearlessness, his earnestness for principles. For years he had had it in mind to retire and write a history of the Civil War period which had been his own period of greatest activity and most intimate acquaintance with the behind-the-scenes of statecraft. Howard's energy, steady application, enthusiasm for journalism and intelligence both as to editorials and as to news made Malcolm look upon him as his natural successor.

"I think Howard is the man we want," he said to his two associates when he was arranging the dinner. "He has new ideas—just what the paper needs. He is in touch with these recent developments. And above all he has judgment. He knows what not to print, where and how to print what ought to be printed. He is still young and is over-enthusiastic. He has limitations, but he knows them and he is eager and capable to learn."

It was a "shop" dinner, Howard doing most of the talking, led on by Malcolm. The main point was the "new journalism," as it was called, and how to adapt it to the *News-Record* and the *News-Record* to it.

Malcolm kept the conversation closely to news and news-ideas, fearing that, if editorial policies were brought in, Howard would make "breaks." He soon saw that his associates were much impressed with Howard, with his judgment, with his knowledge of the details of every important newspaper in the city, with his analysis of the good and bad points in each.

"I'll drop you at your corner," said he to Howard at the end of the dinner. As they drove up the Avenue he began: "How would you like to be the editor of the *News-Record?* My place, I mean."

"I don't understand," Howard answered, bewildered.

"I am going to retire at once," Malcolm went on. "I've been at it nearly fifty years—ever since I was a boy of eighteen and I've been in charge there almost a quarter of a century. I think I've earned a few years of leisure to work for my own amusement. I'm pretty sure they'll want you to take my place. Would you like it?"

"I'm not fit for it," Howard said, and he meant it. "I'm only an apprentice. I'm always making blunders—but I needn't tell you about that."

"You can't say that you are not fit until you have tried. Besides, the question is not, are *you* fit? but, is there any one more fit than you? I confess I don't see any one so well equipped, so certain to give the paper all of the best that there is in him."

"Of course I'd like to try. I can only fail."

"Oh, you won't fail. But you may quarrel with Stokely and Coulter—especially Coulter. In fact, I'm sure you'll quarrel with them. But if you make yourself valuable enough, you'll probably win out. Only——"

Malcolm hesitated, then went on:

"I stopped giving advice years ago. But I'll venture a suggestion. Whenever your principles run counter to the policy of the paper, it would be wise to think the matter over carefully before making an issue. Usually there is truth on both sides, much that can be said fairly and honestly for either side. Often devotion to principle is a mere prejudice. Often the crowd, the mob, can be better controlled to right ends by conceding or seeming to concede a principle for the time. Don't strike a mortal blow at your own usefulness to good causes by making yourself a hasty martyr to some fancied vital principle that will seem of no consequence the next morning but one after the election."

"I know, Mr. Malcolm, judgment is all but impossible. And I have been trying to learn what you have been teaching me with your blue pencil, what you now put into words. But there is something in me—

an instinct, perhaps—that forces me on in spite of myself. I've learned to curb and guide it to a certain extent, but as long as I am I, I shall never learn to control it. Every man must work out his own salvation along his own lines. And with my limitations of judgment, it would be fatal to me, I feel, to study the art of compromise. Where another, broader, stronger, more master of himself and of others, would succeed by compromising, I should fail miserably. I should be lost, compassless, rudderless. I have often envied you your calmness, your ability to see not only to-morrow but the day after. But, if I ever try to imitate you, I shall make a sad mess of my career."

As he ended Howard looked uneasily at the old editor, expecting to see that caustic smile with which he preceded and accompanied his sarcasms at "sentimental bosh." But instead, Malcolm's face was melancholy; and his voice was sad and weary as he answered the young man who was just starting where he had started so many years ago:

"No doubt you are right. I'm not intending to try to dissuade you from—from the best there is in you. All I mean is that caution, self-examination, self-doubt, calm consideration of the other side—these are as necessary to success as energy and resolute action. All I suggest is that its splendour does not redeem a splendid folly. Its folly remains its essential characteristic."

Three weeks later Howard became editor-in-chief of the *News-Record.* His salary was fifteen thousand a year; and Stokely and Coulter, acting upon Malcolm's advice, gave him a "free hand" for one year. They agreed not to interfere during that time unless the circulation or the profits showed a decrease at the end of a quarter.

The next morning Howard, in the Madison Avenue car on his way to the office, read among the "Incidents in Society:"

Mrs. George Alexander Provost and her niece, Miss Marion Trevor, sailed in the *Campania* yesterday. They will return in July for the Newport season.

XV.

YELLOW JOURNALISM.

WHILE several of the New York dailies were circulating from two to three hundred thousand copies, the *News-Record*—the best-written, the most complete, and, where the interests of the owners did not interfere, the most accurate—circulated less than one hundred thousand. The Sunday edition had a circulation of one hundred and fifty thousand where two other newspapers had almost half a million.

The theory of the *News-Record* staff was that their journal was too "respectable," too intelligent, to be widely read; that the "yellow journals" grovelled, "appealed to the mob," drew their vast crowds by the methods of the fakir and the freak. They professed pride in the *News-Record's* smaller circulation as proof of its freedom from vulgarity and debasement. They looked down upon the journalists of the popular newspapers and posed as the aristocracy of the profession.

Howard did not assent to these self-complacent excuses. He was democratic and modern, and the aristocratic pose appealed only to his sense of humour and his suspicions. He believed that the success of the "yellow journals" with the most intelligent, alert and progressive public in the world must be based upon solid reasons of desert, must be in spite of, not because of, their follies and exhibitions of bad taste. He resolved upon a radical departure, a revolution from the policy of satisfying petty vanity and tradition within the office to a policy of satisfying the demands of the public.

He gave Segur temporary charge of the editorial page, and, taking a desk in the news-room, centred his attention upon news and the news-staff. But he was careful not to agitate and antagonise those whose coöperation was necessary to success. He made only one change in the management; he retired old Bowring on a pension and appointed to the city editorship one of the young reporters—Frank Cumnock.

He chose Cumnock for this position, in many respects the most important on the staff of a New York daily, because he wrote well, was a judge of good writing, had a minute knowledge of New York and its neighbourhood and, finally and chiefly, because he had a "news-sense," keener than that of any other man on the paper.

For instance, there was the murder of old Thayer, the rich miser in East Sixteenth Street. It was the sensation in all the newspapers for two weeks. Then they dropped it as an unsolvable mystery. Cumnock persuaded Mr. Bowring to let him keep on. After five days' work he heard of a deaf and dumb woman who sat every afternoon at a back window of her flat overlooking the back windows of Thayer's house. He had a trying struggle with her infirmity and stupidity, but finally was rewarded. On the afternoon of the murder, in its very hour (which the police had been able to discover), she had seen a man and woman in the bathroom of the Thayer house. Both were agitated and the man washed his hands again and again, carefully rinsing the bowl afterward. From her description Cumnock got upon the track of Thayer's niece and her husband, found the proof of their guilt, had them watched until the *News-Record* came out with the "beat," then turned them over to the police.

Also, Cumnock was keen at taking hints of good news-items concealed in obscure paragraphs. The Morris Prison scandal was an example of this. He found in the New England edition of *The World* a six-line item giving an astonishing death rate for the Morris Prison. He asked the City Editor to assign him to go there; and within a week the press of the entire country was discussing the *News-Record's* exposure of the barbarities of torture and starvation practised by Warden Johnson and his keepers.

"We are going to print the news, all the news and

nothing but the news," Howard said to Cumnock. "They've put you here because, so they tell me, you know news no matter how thoroughly it is concealed or disguised. And I assure you that no one shall interfere with you. No favours to anybody; no use of the news-columns for revenge or exploitation. The only questions a news-item need raise in your mind are: Is it true? Is it interesting? Is it printable in a newspaper that will publish anything which a healthy-minded grown-person wishes to read?"

"Is that 'straight'?" asked Cumnock. "No favourites? No suppressions? No exploitations?"

"'Straight'—'dead straight'! And if I were you I'd make this particularly clear to the Wall Street and political men. If anybody"—with stress upon the anybody—"comes to you about this, send him to me."

Howard was uneasy about the managing editor, Mr. King. But he soon found that his fears were groundless. Mr. King was without petty vanity, and cordially and sincerely welcomed his control.

"We look too dull," King began when Howard asked him if he had any changes to suggest. "We need more and bigger headlines, and we need pictures."

"That is it!" Howard was delighted to find that King and he were in perfect accord. "But we must not have pictures unless we can have the best. Just at present we can't increase expenses by any great amount. What do you say to trying what we can do with all the news, larger headlines and plenty of leads?"

"I'm sure we can do better with our class of readers by livening up the appearance of our headlines than we could with second-rate pictures."

"I hope," Howard said earnestly, "that we won't have to use that phrase—'our class of readers'—much longer. Our paper should interest every man and woman able to read. It seems to me that a newspaper's audience should be like that of a good play—the orchestra chairs full and the last seat in the gallery taken. I suppose you know we're not an 'organ' any longer?"

"No, I didn't." Mr. King looked surprised. "Do you mean to say that we're free to print the news?"

"Free as freedom. In our news columns we're neither Democrat nor Republican nor Mugwump nor Reform. We have no Wall Street or social connections. We are going to print a newspaper—all the news and nothing but the news."

Mr. King drummed on his desk softly with the tips of his outstretched fingers. "Hum—hum," he said. "This *is* news. Well—the circulation'll go up. And that's all I'm interested in."

Howard went about his plans quietly. He avoided every appearance of exerting authority, disturbed not a wheel in the great machine. He made his changes so subtly that those who received the suggestions often came to him a few days afterward, proposing as their own the very plans he had hinted. He was thus cautious partly because of his experience of the vanity of men, their sensitiveness to criticism, their instinctive opposition to improvement from without; partly from his knowledge of the hysteria which raged in the offices of the "yellow journals." He wished to avoid an epidemic of that hysteria—the mad rush for sensation and novelty; the strife of opposing ambitions; the plotting and counter-plotting of rival heads of departments; the chaos out of which the craziest ideas often emerged triumphant, making the pages of the paper look like a series of disordered dreams.

He was indifferent to the semblance of authority, to the shadows for which small men are forever struggling. What he wanted, all he wanted, was—results.

The first opposition came from the night editor, who for twenty-six years, his weekly "night off" and his two weeks' vacation in summer excepted, had "made up" the paper—that is to say, had defined, with the advice and consent of the managing editor, the position and order of the various news items. This night editor, Mr. Vroom, was a strenuous conservative. He believed that an editor's duty was done when he had intelligently arranged his paper so that the news was placed before the reader in the order of its importance. Big headlines, attempts at effect with varying sizes of large type and varying column-widths he held to be crowd-catching devices, vulgar and debasing. He had no sympathy with Howard's theory that the first object of a newspaper published in a democratic republic is to catch the crowd, to interest it, to compel it to read, and so to lead it to think.

"We're on the way to scuffling in the gutter with the 'yellow journals' for the pennies of the mob," he was saying sarcastically to Mr. King, one afternoon just as Howard joined them.

Howard laughed. "Not on the way to the gutter, Mr. Vroom. Actually in the gutter, actually scuffling."

"Well, I'm frank to say that I don't like it. A newspaper ought to appeal to the intelligent."

"To intelligence, yes; to the intelligent, no. At least in my opinion, that is the right theory. We want people to read us because we're intelligent enough to know how to please them, not because they're intelligent enough to overcome the difficulties we put in their way. But let's go out to dinner this evening and talk it over."

They dined together at Mouquin's every night for a week. At the end of that time Vroom, still sarcastic and grumbling, was a convert. And a great accession Howard found him. He had sound judgment as to the value of news-items—what demanded first page, the "show-window," because it would interest everybody; what was worth a line on an inside page because it would interest only a few thousands. He was the most skillful of the *News-Record's* many good writers of headlines, a master of that, for the newspaper, art of arts—condensed and interesting statement, alluring the glancing reader to read on. Also he had an eye for effects with type. "You make every page a picture," Howard said to him. "It is wonderful how you balance your headlines, emphasising the important news yet saving the minor items from obscurity. I should like to see the paper you would make if you had the right sort of illustrations to put in."

Vroom was amazed at himself. He who had opposed any "head" which broke the column rule was now so far degenerated into a "yellow journalist" that, when Howard spoke of illustrations, he actually longed to test his skill at distributing them effectively.

* * * * * * * *

Two months of hard work, tedious, because necessarily so indirect, produced a newspaper which was "on the right lines," as Howard understood right lines. And he felt that the time had come to make the necessary radical changes in the editorial page.

The *News-Record* had long posed as independent because it supported now one political party and now the other, or divided its support. But this superficial independence was in reality subservience to the financial interests of the two principal owners. They made their newspaper assail Republican or Democratic corruption and misgovernment in city, state or nation, according as their personal interests lay. They used the editorial page and, to even better advantage, the news-columns, in revenging themselves for too heavy levies of blackmail upon their corrupt interests or in securing unjust legislation and privileges.

Obedient and cynical Mr. Malcolm had made the editorial page corrupt and brilliant—never so effective as when assailing a good cause. The great misfortune of good causes is that they attract so many fatal friends—the superciliously conscientious; the well-meaning but feeble-minded and blundering; the most offensive because least deceptive kinds of hypocrites. Mr. Malcolm, as acute as he was intellectually unscrupulous, well understood how to weaken or to ruin a just cause through these supporters. Sometimes he stood afar off, showering the poisoned arrows of raillery and satire. Again he was the plain-spoken friend of the cause and warned its honest supporters against these "fool friends" whom he pretended to regard as its leaders. Again he played the part of a blind enthusiast and praised folly as wisdom and urged it on to more damaging activities.

"We abhor humbug here," he used to say; and perhaps he did in a measure excuse himself to his conscience with the phrase. But in fact his editorial page was usually a succession of humbugs, of brilliant hypocrisies and cheats perpetrated under the guise of exposing humbug.

Just as Howard was ready to reverse Malcolm's editorial programme, New York was seized with one of its "periodic spasms of virtue." The city government was, as usual, in the hands of the two bosses who owned the two political machines. One was taking the responsibility and the larger share of the spoils; the other was maintaining him in power and getting the smaller but a satisfactory share. The alliance between the police and criminal vice had become so open and aggressive under this bi-boss patronage that the people were aroused and indignant. But as they had no capable leaders and no way of selecting leaders, there arose a self-constituted leadership of uptown Phariseeism and sentimentality, planning the "purification" of the city.

Every man of sense knowing human nature and the

conditions of city life knew that this plan was foredoomed to ridiculous failure, and that the event would be a popular revulsion against "reform."

"Why not speak the truth about these vice-hunters?" Howard was discussing the situation with three of his editorial writers—Segur, Huntington and Montgomery.

"It's mighty dangerous," Montgomery objected. "You will be sticking knives into a sacred Anglo-Saxon hypocrisy."

"Yes, we'll have all the good people about our ears," said Segur. "We'll be denounced as a defender of depravity, a foe of purity. They'll thunder away at us from every pulpit. The other newspapers will take it up, especially those that expect to sell millions of papers containing accounts of the 'exposure' of the dives and dens."

"That's good. I hope we shall," said Howard cheerfully. "It will advertise us tremendously."

The three were better pleased than they would have admitted to themselves by the seeming certainty of Howard's impending undoing.

"No, gentlemen," Howard said, as they were about to go to their rooms for the day's work. "There's no danger in attacking any hypocrisy. Don't attack beliefs that are universal or nearly universal—at least not openly. But don't be afraid of a hypocrisy because it is universal. People know that they are hypocrites in respect of it. They may not have the courage publicly to applaud you. But they'll be privately delighted and will admire your courage. We'll try to be discreet and we'll be careful to be truthful. And we'll begin by making these gentlemen show themselves up."

The next morning the *News-Record* published a double-leaded editorial. It described the importance of improving political and social conditions in New York; it went on to note the distinguished names on the committee for the destruction of vice; it closed with the announcement that on the following day the *News-Record* would publish the views of these eminent reformers upon conditions and remedies.

The next day he printed the interviews—a collection of curiosities in utopianism, cant, ignorant fanaticism, provincialism, hypocrisy. These appeared strictly as news; for the cardinal principle of Howard's theory of a newspaper was that it had no right to intrude its own views into its news-columns. On the editorial page he riddled the interviews. By adroit quotations, by contrasting one with another, he showed, or rather made the so-called reformers themselves show, that where they were sincere they were in the main silly, and where they were plausible they were in the main insincere; that every man of them had his own pet scheme for the salvation of wicked New York; and that they could not possibly accomplish anything more valuable than leading the people on the familiar, aimless, demoralizing excursion through the slums.

On the following day he frankly laughed at them as a lot of impracticables who either did not know the patent facts of city life or refused to admit those facts. And he turned his attention to the real problem, a respectable administration for the city—a practical end which could easily be accomplished by practical action. From day to day he kept this up, publishing a splendid series of articles, humorous, witty, satirical, eloquent, bold, with a dominant strain of sincerity and plain common sense. As his associates had predicted, a storm gathered and burst in fury about the *News-Record*. It was denounced by "leading citizens," including many of the clergy. Its "esteemed" contemporaries published and endorsed and amplified the abuse. And its circulation went up at the rate of five thousand a day.

When the storm was at its height, when the whole town seemed to be agreeing with the angry reformers but was quietly laughing at their folly and hypocrisy, Howard threw his bomb. On a Saturday morning he gave half of his first page with big but severely impartial headlines to an analysis of the members of the vice committee—a broadside of facts often hinted but never before verified and published. First came those who owned property and sub-let it for vicious purposes, the property and purpose specified in detail; then those who were directors in corporations which had got corrupt privileges from the local boss, the privileges being carefully specified, and also the amounts of which they had robbed the city. Last came those who were directors in corporations which had bought from the State-boss injustices and licenses to rob, the specifications given in damning detail.

His leading editorial was entitled "Why We Don't Have Decent Government." It was powerful in its simplicity, its merciless raillery and irony; and only at the very end did it contain passion. There, in a few eloquent sentences he arraigned these professed reformers who were growing rich through the boss-system, who were trafficking with the bosses and were now engaged in wrecking the hopes of honesty and decency. On that day the *News-Record's* circulation went up thirty thousand. The town rang with its "exposure" and the attention of the whole country was arrested. It was one of the historic "beats" of New York journalism. The reputation of the *News-Record* for fearlessness and truth-telling and news-enterprise was established. At a bound it had become the most conspicuous and one of the most powerful journals in New York.

XVI.

MR. STOKELY IS TACTLESS.

HOWARD, riding in the Park one morning late in the spring, came upon Mrs. Carnarvon. She gave him no chance to evade her, but joined him and accommodated her horse's pace to his.

"And are you still on the *News-Record?*" she said. "I hope not."

"Why?" Howard was smiling, glad to get an outside view of what he had been doing.

"Because it's become so sensational. It used to be such a nice paper. And now—gracious, what headlines! What attacks on the very best people in the town!"

"Dreadful, isn't it?" laughed Howard. "We've become so depraved that we are actually telling the truth about somebodies instead of only about nobodies."

"I might have known that you would sympathise with that sort of thing." Mrs. Carnarvon was teasing, yet reproachful. "You always were an anarchist."

"Is it anarchistic to be no respecter of persons and to put big headlines over big items and little headlines over little items?"

"Oh, you know what I mean. You are encouraging the unruly classes."

"Dear me! And we thought we were fighting the unruly class. We thought that it was our friends —or rather, your friends—the franchise grabbers and legislature-buyers who won't obey the laws unless the laws happen to suit their convenience. They're the only unruly class I know anything about. I've heard of another kind but I've never been able to find it. And I never hear much about it except when a lot of big rascals are making off weighted down with plunder. They always shout back over their shoulders: 'Don't raise a disturbance or you'll arouse the unruly classes.'"

Mrs. Carnarvon was laughing. "You put it well," she said, "and I'm not clever enough to answer you. But they all tell me the *News-Record* has become a dangerous paper, that it's attacking everybody who has anything."

"Anything he has stolen, yes. But that's all."

"You can't get me to sympathise with you. I like well-dressed, well-mannered people who speak good English."

"So do I. That's why I'm doing all in my power to improve the conditions for making more and more people of the sort one likes to talk to and dine with."

"Why, I thought you sympathised with the lower classes."

"Not a bit of it. Who has been maligning me to you? I abhor the lower classes—so much so that I wish to see them abolished."

"Well, you'll have to blame Marian for misleading me."

"Miss Trevor? How is she?" Mrs. Carnarvon was looking closely at him, and he was not sure that he succeeded in showing nothing more than friendly interest.

"Haven't you heard from her? She's in England, visiting in Lancashire. You know her cousin married Lord Cranmore."

"I saw in the papers several months ago that she was going abroad. I haven't heard a word since."

Mrs. Carnarvon started to say something, but changed her mind.

"When is she coming home?"

"Not until July. You must come to see us at Newport."

"Nothing could please me better—if I can get away."

"I'll send you an invitation, although you have treated me very badly of late. But I suppose you are busy."

"Busy? Isn't a galley slave always busy?"

"Are you still writing editorials?"

"Yes—and on the fallen *News-Record*. In fact——"

"Well—what?"

Howard laughed. "Don't faint," he said. "I'll leave you at once if you wish me to, and I'll never give it away that you once knew me. I'm the editor—the responsible devil for the depravity."

"How interesting!" Mrs. Carnarvon was evidently not disturbed. Then the American adoration of success came out. "I'm so glad you're getting on. I always knew you would. Really, you must come to dinner. I'll invite some of the people you've been attacking. They'll like to look at you, and you will be amused by them. And I don't in the least mind your giving it to them if they bait you, as I did this morning. Will you come?"

"If I may leave by ten o'clock. I go down town every night."

"Why, when do you sleep?"

"Not much, these days. Life's too interesting to permit of much sleep. I'll make up when it slackens a bit."

As he was turning his horse, she said: "Marian's address is Claridge's, Brooke Street, Mayfair. If she isn't there, they forward her mail."

Howard was puzzled. "What made her give me that address?" he thought. "I know she didn't like my seeing so much of Marian. And here she is practically inviting me to write to her." He could not understand it. "If I were not a 'yellow' editor and if Marian were not engaged to one of the richest men in New York, I'd say that this lady was encouraging me." He smiled. "Not yet—not just yet." And he cheerfully urged his horse into a canter.

Mrs. Carnarvon's opinion of the *News-Record* and its recent performances fairly represented that of the fashionable and the very rich. They read it, as they never did before, because it interested them. They could not deny that what it said was true; that is, they could not deny it to their own minds, although they did vigorously deny it publicly. Those who were attacked directly or indirectly, or expected to be attacked, denounced the paper as an "outrage," a "disgrace to the city," a "specimen of the journalism of the gutter." Many who were not in sympathy with the men or the methods assailed thought that its course was "inexpedient," "tended to increase discontent among the lower classes," "weakened the influence of the better classes." Only a few of the "triumphant classes" saw the real value and benefit of the *News-Record's* frank attacks upon greed and hypocrisy, saw that these attacks were not dangerous or demagogical because they were just and were combined with a careful avoidance of encouragement to the lazy, the envious, the incompetent and the ignorant.

Fortunately for Howard's peace, that eminent New York "multi," Samuel Jocelyn, for whom Coulter had the highest respect, was of this last class. When Howard began, Coulter was at Aiken where Jocelyn had a cottage. He had never been able to make headway with Jocelyn, and Mrs. Jocelyn deigned to give him and Mrs. Coulter only the coldest of cold nods. Just as Coulter had become so agitated by Howard's radical course that he was preparing to go to New York to remonstrate with him, Jocelyn called.

"I came to thank you for what you are doing with your paper," he said cordially. "It seems to me that all intelligent men who are not blind to their own ultimate interests ought to stand by you. I can't tell you how much I admire your frankness and honesty. And you draw the line just right. You attack plunder, you defend property. Will your wife and you dine with us this evening?"

Coulter postponed his trip to New York.

On the last day of the first three months the circulation of the *News-Record* was 147,253—an increase of 42,150 over what it was on the day Howard took charge; its advertising had increased twelve per cent; its net profits for the quarter were seventy-five thousand dollars as against fifty-seven thousand for the preceding quarter.

"Very good indeed," was Stokely's comment.

"Another quarter like this," said Howard, "and I'm going to ask you to let me increase expenses a thousand dollars a week to illustrate the paper."

"We'll talk that over with Coulter. Personally I like this 'yellow-journalism'—when it's done intelligently. I always told Coulter we'd have to come to it. It's only common sense to make a paper easy reading. Then, too, we can have a great deal more influence—in fact, we have already. I'm getting what I want up at Albany this winter much cheaper."

Howard winced. "He made me feel like a blackmailer," he said to himself when Stokely had gone. "And I suppose these fellows do look on me as a new Malcolm with up-to-date tricks. Well, they will see, they will see."

He tried to go on with his work, but Stokely's cynical words persistently interrupted him. Why had he not squarely challenged Stokely then and there? Why had he only winced where a year ago he would have demanded an explanation?

He hated to confess it to himself, he made every effort to smother it, but the thought still stared him in the face—"I am not so strong in my ideals of personal character as I was a year ago."

The fact that his present course was profitable gave him, he felt, more pleasure than the fact that it was right. If the alternative of wealth and power with self-abasement or poverty, obscurity with self-respect were put to him now, what would he decide? Would he give up his prospects, his hopes of Marian and of an easy career? He was afraid to answer. He contented himself with one of his habitual evasions—"I will settle that when the time comes. No, Stokely's remark did not make a crisis. If the crisis ever does come, surely I will act like a man. I'll be securer then, more necessary to this pair of plunderers, able to make better terms for myself. In practical life, it is necessary to sacrifice something in order to succeed."

But Stokely's words and his own silence and the real reasons for his changing ideals and for his cowardice continued to annoy him.

Every day he came down town planning for a better newspaper the next morning than they had ever made before. And his vigour, his enthusiasm permeated the entire office. He went from one news department to another, suggesting, asking for suggestions, praising, criticising judiciously and with the greatest consideration for vanity. He talked with the reporters, urging them on by showing keen interest in them and their work, and intimate knowledge of what they were doing. And he dictated every day telegrams to correspondents, thanking them for any conspicuously good stories they had telegraphed in, adding something to the compensation of those who were paid by space and made little.

If his work had not been his amusement the long hours, the constant application, would have broken him down. But he had no interests outside the office and he got his mental recreation by shifting his mind from one department to another.

In June his salary was increased to twenty-five thousand a year and his last lingering feeling of financial insecurity disappeared. For the first time in his life he felt strong enough to undertake a serious responsibility, to give hostages to fortune without fear of being unable to keep faith. He learned from Mrs. Carnarvon that Marian was returning on the *Oceanic* on the ninth of July, and he accepted a Saturday-to-Monday invitation to Newport for the twelfth of July. It was from Segur that he got the news that Danvers was in Japan and was not returning until the autumn.

On the ninth of July, from the window of his office, he saw the *Oceanic* steam up the bay and up the river to her pier. He sent down a request that the ship-news reporter be sent up as soon as he returned.

"Is it a good story?" he asked when the reporter, Blackwell, entered. "Was there anybody on board?"

"A lot of swell people," the young man answered; "all the women got up in the latest Paris gowns."

"Did you notice whether Mrs. Provost came?"

"Came? Well, rather, with two French maids chattering and chasing after her. And there was a tall girl with her, a stunner, a girl she called 'Marian, my dear.'"

Howard stopped him with "Thank you. Don't write anything about them."

"It was the best thing I saw—the funniest."

"Well—don't use the names."

Young Blackwell turned to go. "Oh, I see—friends of yours," he smiled. "Very well. I'll keep 'em out."

Howard flushed and called him back. "Go ahead," he said. "Write just what you were going to. Of course you wouldn't write anything that was not fair and truthful. We don't 'play favourites' here. Forget what I said."

And so it came to pass that Mrs. Provost, half pleased, half indignant, said to Miss Trevor as they sat in the drawing room of the Pullman on the way to Newport the next day: "Just look at this, Marian dear, in the horrid *News-Record*. And it used to be such a nice paper with that slimy Coulter bowing and scraping to everybody."

"This" was Mrs. Provost and her dogs and her maids and her asides to "Marian dear," described with accuracy and a keen sense of the ludicrous.

"It's too dreadful," she continued. "There is no such thing as privacy in this country. The newspapers are making us," with a slight accent on the pronoun, "as common and public as tenement-house people."

"Yes," Miss Trevor answered absently. "But why read the newspapers? I never could get interested in them, though I've tried."

XVII.

A WOMAN AND A WARNING.

ON the evening of Howard's arrival at Newport, Mrs. Carnarvon was having a few people in to dine. He had just time to dress and so saw no one until he descended to the reception room.

"You are to take in Marian," said his hostess, going with him to where Miss Trevor was sitting, her back to the door and her attention apparently absorbed by the man facing her.

"Here's Mr. Howard, Marian," Mrs. Carnarvon interrupted. "Come with me, Willie. Your lady is over here and we're going in directly."

Marian saw that Howard was looking at her in the straight, frank fashion she remembered and liked so well. "I've come for you," he said.

"Yes, you are to take me in," she evaded, her look even lamer than her words.

"You know what I mean." He was smiling, his heart in his eyes, as if the dozen people were not about them.

"I see you have not changed," she laughed, answering his look in kind.

"Changed? I'm revolutionized. I was blind and now I see. I was paralyzed and behold, I walk. I was weak and lo, I am strong—strong enough for two, if necessary."

"Now, hasn't it occurred to you that I might possibly have something to say about my own fate?"

"You? Why, you had everything to say. I reasoned it all out with you. You simply can't add anything to the case I made you make out for yourself when I talked it over with you. I made you protest very vigorously."

"Well, what did I say—that is, what did you make me say?"

"You said you were engaged—pledged to another—that you could not draw back without dishonour. And I answered that no engagement could bind you to become the wife of a man you did not love; that no moral code could hold you to such a sin; that no code of honour could command you to permit a man to degrade himself and you. Then you pleaded that you were not sure you liked my kind of a life, that you feared you wanted wealth and a great establishment and social leadership and—and all that."

"Did I?" Marian said with exaggerated astonishment.

"You did indeed. You were perfectly open with me. You let me see all that part of you which we try to keep concealed and fancy we are concealing—all that one really feels and wishes and thinks as distinguished from what one fancies he ought to feel and wish and think."

"I wonder that you cared, after a glance behind that curtain."

"Oh, but I like what is behind that curtain best of all. The very human things are there. They make me feel so at home."

Dinner was announced and it was not until the second course that he had a chance to resume. Then he began as if there had been no interval:

"You said——"

Marian laughed and looked at him—a flash of her luminous blue-green eyes—and was looking away again with her usual expression. "You needn't tell me the rest. It doesn't matter what I said. I've had you with me wherever I went. You never doubted my—my caring, did you?"

"No. I couldn't doubt you. If you were the sort of woman a man could doubt, you wouldn't be the sort of woman I could love. And you know it isn't vanity that makes me sure. I often wonder how you happened to care for such a—but I must not attack any one whom you like so well. No, I knew you cared by the same instinct that makes you know that I care for you."

"But why did you come?"

"Because I have won a position for myself, have enough to enable us to live without eternally fretting over money-matters. I feel that I have the right to come. And then I could not be interested to live on, without you; and I'm willing to face, willing to have you face, whatever may come to us through me. I know that you and I together——"

"Not now—don't—please." Marian was pale and she was obviously under a great strain. "You see, you knew all about this. But I didn't until you looked at me when Jessie brought you. It makes me—happy—I am so happy. But I must—I can't control myself here." She leaned over as if her napkin had slipped to the floor. "I love you," she murmured.

It was Howard's turn to struggle for self-control. "I understand," he said, "why you wished me not to go on. You never said those words to me before—and——"

"Oh, yes I have—many and many a time."

"With your eyes, but not with your voice—at least not so that I could hear. And—well, it is not easy to look calm and only friendly when every nerve in one's body is vibrating like a violin string under the bow. Yes, let us talk of something else. I've never been acutely conscious of the presence of others when

I've been with you. To-night I'm in great danger of forgetting them altogether."

"That would be so like you." Marian laughed, then raised her voice a little and went on. "Yes, your little restaurant in the Rue Louis le Grand was gone. There was a dressmaker in its place—Raudinitz. She made this. How do you like it?"

"It has the air of—of belonging to you."

Marian looked amused. Howard shrugged his shoulders. "All roads lead to Rome," he said.

* * * * * * * * *

Carnarvon hung about until the women went to bed, so Howard and Marian had no opportunity to be alone. As soon as he saw his last chance vanish, he went to his own room, to the solitude of its balcony in the shadow of the projecting façade with the moonlight flooding the rocks and the sea.

As he sat smoking, the recession came, the reaction from weeks of nervous tension. And with the ebb of the tide entered that Visitor who alone has the privilege of the innermost chamber where lives the man himself, unmasked of all vanity and show and pretense. The visit was not unexpected; for at every such crisis every one is certain of a call from this Visitor, this merciless critic, plain and rude of speech, rare and reluctant in praise, so mocking in our moments of elation, so cruelly frank about our follies and self-excuses when he comes in our moments of depression.

"So you are going to marry?" the Visitor said abruptly. "I thought you had made up your mind on that subject long ago."

"Love changes a man's point of view," Howard replied, timid and apologetic before this quiet, relentless other-self.

"But it doesn't change the facts of life, does it? It doesn't change character, does it?"

"I think so. For instance, it has changed me. It has made a man of me. It has been the inspiration of the past year, strengthening me, making me ambitious, energetic. Have I not thought of her all the time, worked for her?"

"You have been uncommonly persistent—as you always are when you are thwarted." The Visitor wore a satirical smile. "But a spurt of inspiration is one thing. A wife—responsibility—fetters——"

"Not when one loves."

"That depends upon the kind of love—and the kind of woman—and the kind of man."

"Could there be any higher kind of love than ours?"

"Most romantic, most high-minded—quite idyllic." The Visitor's tone was gently mocking. "And I don't deny that you may go on loving each the other. But —how does she fit in with your scheme of life? What does she really know of or care about your ambitions? Why, you had so little confidence in her that you didn't dare to think of marrying her until you had an income which you once would have thought wealth—an income which, by the way, already begins to seem small to you."

"No, it wasn't lack of confidence in her," protested Howard. "It was lack of confidence in myself."

"True, that did have something to do with it, I grant you. And that reminds me—what has become of all your cowardice about responsibility?"

"Oh, I'm changed there."

"Are you sure? Are you not deceived by this sudden and maybe momentary streak of good luck in your affairs? You have fixed your ambition high—very high. You wish to make an honest and a useful and a distinguished career. You know you have weaknesses. I needn't remind you—need I—that you have had to fight those weaknesses? How could you have won thus far if you had been responsible for others instead of being alone, and certain that the consequences would fall upon yourself only? I want to see you continue to win. I don't want to see you dragged down by extravagance, by love for this woman, by ambition of the kind her friends approve. I don't want to see you—You were silent when Stokely insulted you!"

"Love—such love as mine—and for such a woman—and with such love in return—drag down? Impossible!"

"Not so—not exactly so, though I must say you are plausible. But don't forget that you and she are not starting out to make a career. Don't forget that she is already fixed—her tastes, habits, friendships, associations, ideals already formed. Don't forget that your love is the only bond between you—and that it may drag you toward her mode of life instead of drawing her towards yours. Don't forget that your own associations and temptations are becoming more and more difficult. I repeat, you cringed—yes, cringed—when Stokely insulted you. Why?"

Howard was silent.

"And," the Visitor went on relentlessly, "let me remind you that not only did you give her up without a struggle a few months ago but also she gave you up without a word."

"But what could she have said?"

"I don't know, I'm sure. I'm not familiar with ways feminine. But I know—we know—that, if there had not been some reservation in her love, some hesitation about you—unconscious, perhaps, but powerful enough to make her yield—she would not have let you go as she did."

"But she did not realise, as I did not, how much our love meant to us."

"Perhaps—that sounds well. All I ask is, will she help you? Are you really so much stronger than you were only four months ago? Or are you stimulated by success? Suppose that days of disaster, of peril, come? What then?"

"But they will not. I have won a position. I can always command a large salary—perhaps not quite so much but still a large salary."

"Perhaps—if you don't trouble yourself about principles. But how would it be if you would do nothing, write nothing, except what you think is honest? Would you ask her to face it? Tell me, tell yourself honestly, have you the right to assume a responsibility you may not be able to bear, to invite temptations you may not be able to resist?"

There was a long silence. At last Howard stood up and flung his cigar into the sea. His face was drawn and his eyes burned.

"God in heaven!" he cried, "am I not human? May I not have companionship and sympathy and love? Must I be alone and friendless and loveless always? That is not life; that is not just. I will not; I will not. I love her—love her—love her. With the best that there is in me, I love her. Am I such a coward that I cannot face even my own weaknesses?"

XVIII.

HOWARD EXPLAINS HIS MACHINE.

In August Marian and Mrs. Carnarvon came to the Waldorf for two days. Howard had offered to show them how a newspaper is made; and Mrs. Carnarvon, finding herself bored by too many days of the same few people every day, herself proposed the trip. The three dined in the open air on Sherry's piazza and at eleven o'clock drove down the Avenue, to the east at Washington Square, and through the Bowery.

"I never saw it before," said Marian, "and I must say I shall not care if I never see it again. Why do people make so much fuss about slums, I wonder?"

"Oh, they're so queer, so like another world," suggested Mrs. Carnarvon. "It gives you such a delightful sensation of sadness. It's just like a not-too-melancholy play, only better because it's real. Then, too, it makes one feel so much more comfortable and clean and contented in one's own surroundings."

"You ought to be ashamed of yourself, Jessie." Marian spoke in mock indignation. "The next thing we know you'll sink to being a patron of the poor and go about enjoying yourself at making them self-conscious and envious."

"They're not at all sad down this way," said Howard, "except in the usual inescapable human ways. When they're not hit too hard, they bear up wonderfully. You see, living on the verge of ruin and tumbling over every few weeks get one used to it. It ceases to give the sensation of event."

Their automobile had turned into Park Row and so reached the *News-Record* building in Printing House Square. Howard took the two women to the elevator and they shot upward in a car crowded with telegraph messengers, each carrying one or more envelopes, some of them bearing in bold black type the words: "News!—Rush!"

"I suppose that is the news for the paper?" Mrs. Carnarvon asked.

"A little of it. Our special cable and special news from towns to which we have no direct wire and also the *Associated Press* reports come this way.. But we don't use much *Associated Press* matter, as it is the same for all the papers."

"What do you do with it?"

"Throw it away. A New York newspaper throws away every night enough to fill two papers and often enough to fill five or six."

"Isn't that very wasteful?"

"Yes, but it's necessary. Every editor has his own idea of what to print and what not to print and how much space each news event calls for. It is there that editors show their judgment or lack of it. To print the things the people wish to read in the quantities the people like and in the form the most people can most easily understand—that is success as an editor."

"No doubt," said Marian, thinking of the low view all her friends took of Howard's newspaper, "if you were making a newspaper to please yourself, you would make a very different one."

"Oh, no," laughed Howard, "I print what I myself like; that is, what I like to find in a newspaper. We print human news made by human beings and interesting to human beings. And we don't pretend to be anything more than human. We try never to think of our own idea of what the people ought to read, but always to get at what the people themselves think they ought to read. We are journalists, not news-censors."

"I must say newspapers do not interest me." Marian confessed it a little diffidently.

"You are probably not interested," Howard answered, "because you don't care for news. It is a queer passion—the passion for news. The public has it in a way. But to see it in its delirium you must come here."

"This seems quiet enough." Marian looked about Howard's upstairs office. It was silent, and from the windows one could see New York and its rivers and harbour, vast, vague, mysterious, animated yet quiet.

"Oh, I rarely come here—a few hours a week," Howard replied. "On this floor the editorial writers work." He opened a door leading to a private hall. There were five small rooms. In each sat a coatless man, smoking and writing. One was Segur, and Howard called to him.

"Are you too busy to look after Mrs. Carnarvon and Miss Trevor for a few minutes? I must go down-stairs."

Segur gave some "copy" to a boy who handed him a bundle of proofs and rushed away down a narrow staircase. Howard descended in the elevator, and Segur, who had put on his coat, sat talking to the two women as he looked through the proofs, glancing at each narrow strip, then letting it drop to the floor.

"You don't mind my working?" he asked. "I have to look at these things to see if there is any news that calls for editional attention. If I find anything and can think an editorial thought about it, I write it; and if Howard is in the humour, perhaps the public is permitted to read it."

"Is he severe?" asked Mrs. Carnarvon.

"The 'worst ever,'" laughed Segur. "He is very positive and likes only a certain style and won't have anything that doesn't exactly fit his ideas. He's easy to get along with but difficult to work for."

"I imagine his positiveness is the secret of his success." Marian knew that Segur was half in jest and was fond of Howard. But she couldn't endure hearing him criticised.

"No. I think he succeeds because he works, pushes straight on, never stops to repair blunders but never makes the same kind of a blunder the second time."

Segur's eye caught an item that suggested an editorial paragraph. He sat at Howard's desk, thought a moment, scrawled half a dozen lines in a large ragged hand on a sheet of ruled yellow paper, and pressed an electric button. The boy came, handed him another thick bundle of proofs, took the "copy" and withdrew. Just then Howard returned.

"We'll go down to the news-room," he said.

The windows of the great news-room were thrown wide. Scores of electric lights made it bright. At the various desks or in the aisles were perhaps fifty men, most of them young, none of them beyond middle age. They were in every kind of clothing from the most fashionable summer attire to an old pair of cheap and stained duck trousers, collarless negligee shirt open all the way down the front and suspenders hanging about the hips.

Some were writing long-hand; others were pounding away at the typewriter; others were talking in undertones to "typists" taking dictation to the machine; others were reading "copy" and altering it with huge blue pencils which made apparently unreadable smears wherever they touched the paper. In and out skurried a dozen office-boys, responding to calls from various desks, bringing bundles of proofs, thrusting copy into boxes which instantly and noisily shot up through the ceiling.

It was a scene of confusion and furious activity. The face of each individual was calm and his motions by themselves were not excited. But taking all together and adding the tense, strained expression underneath the calm—the expression of the professional gambler—there was a total of active energy that was oppressive.

"We had a fire below us one night," said Howard. "We are two hundred feet from the street and there were no fire escapes. We all thought it was good-bye. It was nearly half an hour before we found out that the smoke booming up the stairways and into this room had no danger behind it."

"Gracious!" Mrs. Carnarvon shuddered and looked uneasily about.

"It's perfectly safe," Howard reassured her. "We've arranged things better since then. Besides, that fire demonstrated that the building was fireproof."

"And what happened?" asked Miss Trevor.

"Why, just what you see now. The Managing Editor, Mr. King over there—I'll introduce him to you presently—went up to a group of men standing at one of the windows. They were pretending indifference as they looked down at the crowd which was shouting and tossing its arms in a way that more than suggested pity for us poor devils up here. Well, King said: 'Boys, boys, this isn't getting out a paper.' Every one went back to his work and—and that was all."

They went on to the room behind the news-room. As Howard opened its heavy door a sound, almost a roar, of clicking instruments and typewriters burst out. Here again were scores of desks with men seated at them, every man with a typewriter and a telegraph instrument before him.

"These are our direct wires," Howard explained. "Our correspondents in all the big cities, east, west, north and south and in London, are at the other end of these wires. Let me show you."

Howard spoke to the operator nearest them. "Whom have you got?"

"I'm taking three thousand words from Kansas City," he replied. "Washington is on the next wire."

"Ask Mr. Simpson how the President is to-night," Howard said to the Washington operator.

His instrument clicked a few times and was silent. Almost immediately the receiver began to click and, as the operator dashed the message off on his typewriter the two women read over his shoulder: "Just came from White House. He is no better, probably a little worse because weaker. Simpson."

"And can you hear just as quickly from London?" Marian asked.

"Almost. I'll try. There is always a little delay in transmission from the land systems to the cable system; and messages have to be telephoned between our office in Trafalgar Square and the cable office down in the city. Let's see, it's five o'clock in the morning in London now. They've been having it hot there. I'll ask about the weather."

Howard dictated to the man at the London wire: "Roberts, London. How is the weather? Howard."

In less than ten minutes the cable-man handed Howard a typewritten slip reading: "*News-Record*, New York, Howard: Thermometer 97 our office now. Promises hottest day yet. Roberts."

"I never before realised how we have destroyed distance," said Mrs. Carnarvon.

"I don't think any one but a newspaper editor completely realises it," Howard answered. "As one sits here night after night, sending messages far and wide and receiving immediate answers, he loses all sense of space. The whole world seems to be in his anteroom."

"I begin to see fascination in this life of yours." Marian's face showed interest to enthusiasm. "This atmosphere tightens one's nerves. It seems to me that in the next moment I shall hear of some thrilling happening."

"It's listening for the first rumour of the 'about-to happen' that makes newspaper-men so old and yet so young, so worn and yet so eager. Every night, every moment of every night, we are expecting it, hoping for some astounding news which it will test our resources to the utmost to present adequately."

From the news-room they went up to the composing room—a vast hall of confusion, filled with strange-looking machines and half-dressed men and boys. Some were hurrying about with galleys of type, with large metal frames; some were wheeling tables here and there; scores of men and a few women were seated at the machines. These responded to touches upon their key-boards by going through uncanny internal agitations. Then out from a mysterious somewhere would come a small thin strip of almost hot metal, the width of a newspaper column and marked along one edge with letters printed backwards.

Up through the floor of this room burst boxes filled with "copy." Boys snatched the scrawled, ragged-looking sheets and tossed them upon a desk. A man seated there cut them into little strips, hanging each strip upon a hook. A line of men filed rapidly past these hooks, snatching each man a single strip and darting away to a machine.

"It is getting late," said Howard. "The final rush for the first edition is on. They are setting the last 'copy.'"

"But," Mrs. Carnarvon asked, "how do they ever get the different parts of the different news-items together straight?"

"The man who is cutting copy there—don't you see him make little marks on each piece? Those marks tell them just where their 'take,' as they call it, belongs."

They went over to the part of the great room where there were many tables, on each a metal frame about the size of a page of the newspaper. Some of the frames were filled with type, others were partly empty. And men were lifting into them the galleys of type under the direction of the Night Editor and his staff. As soon as a frame was filled two men began to even the ends of the columns and then to screw up an inside framework which held the type firmly in place. Then a man laid a great sheet of what looked like blotting-paper upon the page of type and pounded it down with a mallet and scraped it with a stiff brush.

"That is the matrix," said Howard. "See him putting it on the elevator." They looked down the shaft. "It has dropped to the sub-basement," said Howard, "two hundred and fifty feet below us. They are already bending it into a casting-box of the shape of the cylinders on the presses; metal will be poured in and when it is cool, you will have the metal form, the metal impression of the page. It will be fastened upon the press to print from."

They walked back through the room which was now in almost lunatic confusion—forms being locked; galleys being lifted in; editors, compositors, boys, rushing to and fro in a fury of activity. Again the phenomenon of the news-room, the individual faces calm but their tense expressions and their swift motions making an impression of almost irrational excitement.

"Why such haste?" asked Marian.

"Because the paper must be put to press. It must contain the very latest news and it must also catch the mails; and the mail-trains do not wait."

They descended in the main elevator to the ground floor and then went down a dark and winding staircase until they faced an iron door. Howard pushed it open and they entered the press-room. Its temperature was blood-heat, its air heavy and nauseating with the odours of ink, moist paper and oil, its lights dim. They were in a gallery and below them on all sides were the huge presses, silent, motionless, waiting.

Suddenly a small army of men leaped upon the mighty machines, scrambled over them, then sprang back. With a tremendous roar that shook the entire building the presses began to revolve, to hurl out great heaps of newspapers.

"Those presses eat six hundred thousand pounds of paper and four tons of ink a week," Howard shouted. "They can throw out two hundred thousand complete papers an hour—papers that are cut, folded, pasted, and ready to send away. Let us go before you are stifled. This air is horrible."

They returned in the elevator to his lofty office. Even there a slight vibration from the press-room could be felt. But it was calm and still, a fit place from which to view the panorama of sleeping city and drowsy harbour tranquil in the moonlight.

"Look." Howard was leaning over the railing just outside his window.

They looked straight down three hundred feet to the street made bright by electric lights. Scores of wagons loaded with newspapers were rushing away from the several newspaper buildings. The shouts, the clash of hoofs and heavy tires on the granite blocks, the whirr of automobiles, were borne faintly upward.

"It is the race to the railway stations to catch the mail-trains," Howard explained. "The first editions go to the country. These wagons are hurrying in order that tens of thousands of people hundreds of miles away, at Boston, Philadelphia, Washington and scores on scores of towns between and beyond, may find the New York newspapers on their breakfast-tables."

The office-boy came with a bundle of papers, warm, moist, the ink brilliant.

"And now for the inquest," said Howard.

"The inquest?" Marian looked at him inquiringly.

"Yes—viewing the corpse. It was to give birth to this that there was all that intensity and fury—that and a thousand times more. For, remember, this paper is the work of perhaps twenty thousand brains, in every part of the world, throughout civilisation and far into the depths of barbarism. Look at these date lines—cities and towns everywhere in our own country, Canada, Mexico, Central America, South America. You'll find most of the capitals of Europe represented; and Africa, north, south and central, east and west coast. Here's India and here the heart of Siberia.

There is China and there Japan and there Australia. Think of these scores of newspaper correspondents telegraphing news of the doings of their fellow beings —not what they did last month or last year, but what they did a few hours ago—some of it what they were doing while we were dining up at Sherry's. Then think of the thousands on thousands of these newspaper-men, eager, watchful agents of publicity, who were on duty but had nothing to report to-day. And——"

Howard shrugged his shoulders and tossed the paper from him.

"There it lies," he said, "a corpse. Already a corpse, its life ended before it was fairly born. There it is, dead and done for—writ in water, and by anonymous hands. Who knows who did it? Who cares?"

He caught Marian's eyes, looking wonder and reproach.

"I don't like to hear you say that," she said, forgetting Mrs. Carnarvon. "Other men—yes, the little men who work for the cheap rewards. But not you, who work for the sake of work. This night's experience has thrilled me. I understand your profession now. I see what it means to us all, to civilisation, what a splendid force for good, for enlightenment, for uplifting it is. I can see a great flood of light radiating from this building, pouring into the dark places, driving away ignorance. And the thunder of those presses seems to me to fill the world with some mighty command—what is it?—oh, yes—I can hear it distinctly. It is, 'Let there be light!'"

Mrs. Carnarvon's back was toward them and she was looking out at the harbour. Howard put his hands upon Marian's shoulders and they looked each the other straight in the eyes.

"Lovers and comrades," he said, "always. And how strong we are—together!"

XIX.

"I MUST BE RICH."

"WHILE I don't feel dependent upon the owners of the *News-Record*, still I am not exactly independent of them either. And if I left them it would only be to become dependent in the same way upon somebody else. A man who makes his living by the advocacy of principles should be wholly free. If he isn't, the principles are sure sooner or later to become incidental to the living, instead of the living being incidental to the principles."

"But you see—perhaps I ought to have told you before—that is, there may be"—Marian was stammering and blushing.

"What's the matter? Don't frighten me by looking so—so criminal," Howard laughed.

It was late in August. Marian was visiting Mrs. Brandon at Irvington-on-the-Hudson and she and Howard were driving.

"I never told you. But the fact is"—she hesitated again.

"Is it about your other engagement? You never told me about that—how you broke it off. I don't want you to tell me unless you wish to. You know I never meddle in past matters. I'm simply trying to help you out."

"Instead, you're making it worse. I'd rather not tell you that if——"

"We'll never speak of it again. And now, what is it that is troubling you?"

"I have been trying to tell you—I wish you wouldn't look at me—I've got a small income—it's really very small."

"I'm glad to hear it."

"I was afraid you wouldn't like it. It isn't very big—only about eight thousand a year—some years not so much. But then, if anything happened—we could be—we could live."

Howard smiled as he looked at her—but not with his eyes.

"I'm glad," he said. "It makes me feel safer in several ways. And I'm especially glad that it is not larger than mine. I know it's stupid, as so many of our instincts are; but I should not like to marry a woman who had a larger income than I could earn. I think it is the only remnant I have of the 'lord and master' idea that makes so many men ridiculous. But we need not let that bother us. Fate has made us about equal in this respect, so unimportant yet so important; and we are each independent of the other.

Each will always know that love is the only bond that holds us together."

They decided that they would live at the rate of about fifteen thousand a year and would put by the rest of their income. She was to undertake the entire management of their home, he transferring his share by check each month.

"And so," she said, "we shall never have to discuss money matters."

"We couldn't," laughed Howard. "I don't know anything about them and could not take part in a discussion."

As they were to be married in November, they planned to take an apartment when Marian came back to town—in late September. She was to attend to the furnishing and all was to be in readiness by the time they were married. Howard was to get a six weeks' vacation and, as soon as they returned, they were to go to housekeeping.

Her visit to the *News-Record* office had made a change in her. Until she met Howard, she had known only the world-that-idles and the world-that-drudges. Howard brought her the first real news of the world-that-works. Of course she knew that there was such a world, but she had confused it with the world-that-drudges. She liked to hear Howard talk about his world, but she thought that his enthusiasm blinded him to the truth of its drudgery; and she often caught her self half regretting that he had to work.

But that vast machine for the swift collecting and distributing of the news of the world had opened her eyes, had made her see her lover and, through him, his life, in a different aspect. She had accepted the supercilious, thoughtless opinion of those about her that the newspaper is a mere purveyor of inaccurate gossip. And while Howard had tried to show her his profession as it was, he had only succeeded in convincing her that he himself had an exalted view of it; a view which she thought creditable to him but wide of the disagreeable truth.

On that trip down-town she had seen "the press" with the flaws reduced and the merits looming. She had looked into those all-seeing eyes that watch the councils of statesmen and the movements of nations and peoples, yet also note the swing of a murderous knife in an alley of the slums. She had heard that stentorian voice of Publicity, arousing the people of the earth to apprehend, to reflect, to progress.

She had been proud of Howard for his appearance, for what he said and the way he said it. Now she was proud of him for the part he was taking in this wonderful world-that-works. And she would not have confessed to him how insignificant she felt, how weak and worthless.

She thought she was impatient for the time to come when she could learn how to help him in his work, could begin to feel that she too had a real share in it. With what seemed to her most creditable energy and self-sacrifice she tried again to interest herself in newspapers. But the trivial parts bored her; the chronicles of crime repelled her; and the politics and most of the other serious articles were beyond the range of her knowledge or of her interest. "I shall wait until we are married," she said, "then he will teach me." And she did not suspect how significant, how ominous her postponement was.

She asked him if he would not teach her and he replied: "Why, certainly, if you are interested. But I don't intend to trouble you with the details of my profession. I want you to lead your own life—to do what interests you."

She did not stop to analyse her feeling of relief at this release, and went on to protest: "But I want your life to be my life. I want there to be only one life—our life."

"And there shall be—each contributing his share, at least I'll try to contribute mine. But you have your own individuality, dear; and a very strong one it is. And I don't want you to change."

At the time he was deep in his plans for illustrating the *News-Record*. Early in that fall's campaign they had secured the best cartoonist in America. Cartoons are rarely the work of one man but are got up by consultations. Howard spent never less than an hour each day with the cartoonist, Wickham, wrestling with the problem of the next day's picture. For he insisted upon having a striking cartoon each day, and gave it the most conspicuous place in the paper—the top-centre of the first page.

"If a cartoon is worth printing at all," he said, "it is worth printing large and conspicuous. And to be worth printing it must be like an ideal editorial—one point sharply and swiftly made and so clear that the most careless glance-of-the-eye is enough."

Wickham had made a series of cartoons on the campaign, humorous and satirical, which had the distinction of being reproduced on lantern slides for use in all parts of the town. It was an admirable beginning of the new policy of illustration. Howard had been making a careful study of all the illustrators in the country, not overlooking those toiling in obscurity on the big western dailies. He had selected a staff of twenty; as soon as Coulter and Stokely assented, he engaged them by telegraph. Five were developed artists, the rest beginners with talent. He gave all of his attention for two weeks to organising this staff. He infected it with his enthusiasm. He impressed upon it his ideas of newspaper illustration—the dash and energy of the French illustrators adapted to American public taste. He insisted upon the artists studying the French illustrated papers and applying what they learned. It was not until the first Sunday in December that he felt ready to submit the results of these labours to the public.

Again he scored over the "contemporaries" of the *News-Record.* They printed many more illustrations than it did. It had only one illustration on a page, but there was one on every page and a good one. All the subjects were well chosen—either action or character—and as many good looking women as possible.

"Never publish a commonplace face," he said. "There is no such thing in life as an uninteresting face. Always find the element of interest and bring it out."

The result of this policy, interpreted by a carefully trained and enthusiastic staff, was what the out-of-town press was soon praising as "a revelation in newspaper-illustration." Howard himself was surprised. He had mentally insured against a long period of disappointment.

"This shows," he remarked to King and Vroom, "how much more competent men are than we usually think—if they get a chance, if they are pointed in the right direction and are left free."

"He certainly knows his business." Vroom was

looking after Howard admiringly. "I never saw anybody who so well understood when to lead and when to let alone. What results he does get!"

"A pity to waste such talents on this thankless business," said King. "If he'd gone into real business, he would have a salary of a hundred thousand a year, would be rich and secure for life. Why, a business man could and would make a whole career on the ideas he has in a single week. As it is——"

King shrugged his shoulders and Vroom finished the sentence for him: "Coulter and Stokely could kick him out to-morrow and the *News-Record* would go straight on living upon his ideas for ten years at least."

Howard needed no one to make this truth clear to him to the full. Often, as he thought of his expanding tastes, his expanding expenditures and his expanding plans both for his private life and for his career, he felt an awful sinking at the heart and a sense of fundamental weakness.

"I am building upon sand," he said to himself. "In business, in the law, in almost any other career to-day's work would be to-morrow's capital. As it is, I am ever more and more a slave. To be free I ought to be poor or rich. And I cannot endure the thought of poverty again. I must be rich."

The idea allured him to a degree that made him ashamed of himself. Sometimes, when he was talking to Marian or writing editorials, all in the strain of high principle and contempt for sordidness, he would flush at the thought that he was in reality a good deal of a hypocrite. "I'm expressing the ideals I ought to have, the ideals I used to have, not the ideals I have."

But the clearer this discrepancy became to him and the wider the gap between what he ought to think and what he really did think, the more strenuously he protested to himself against himself, and the more fiercely he denounced in public the very poison he was himself taking.

"I am living in a tainted atmosphere," he said to Marian. "We all are. I fight against the taint but how can I hope to avoid the consequences if I persist in breathing it, in absorbing it at every pore of my body?"

"I don't understand you." Marian was used to his moods of self-criticism and did not attach much importance to them.

He thought a moment. "Oh, nothing," he said. "What's the use of discussing what can't be helped?" How could he tell her that the greatest factor in his enervating environment was herself; that the strongest chains which held him in it were the chains which bound him to her? Indeed, was he not indulging in cowardly self-excuse in thinking that this was true? Had not his success, rather than his love, made ambition unfettered by principle the mainspring of his life?

XX.

ILLUSION.

"HOW shall we be married?" Howard asked her in the late Autumn.

"I know it will not be in a church with ushers and bridesmaids and a crowd gaping at us. I suppose there is a public side to marriage since the state makes one enter into a formal contract. But that can be done privately. I should as soon think of driving down the Avenue with my arms about your neck as of a public wedding."

"Thank you," he laughed. "I was afraid—well, women are usually so fond of—but you're not usual. Let us see. The minister is absolutely necessary, I suppose. Would one feel married if there were not a minister?"

"I don't know—I feel——"

She hesitated and blushed but looked straight at him with that expression in her eyes which always made him think of their love as their religion.

"Feel—go on. I want to hear that very, very much."

"I feel as if I were just as much married to you now as I ever could be."

"And that is how I have felt ever since the day, when I hardly knew you, when you suddenly came into my life—my real, inner life where no one had been before—and sat down and at once made it look as if it were your home. And the place that had been lonely was lonely no more, and has not been since."

She put her hand in his and he saw that there were tears in her eyes.

"What is it?" he asked.

"Only that—that I am so happy. It—it frightens me. It seems so like a dream."

"It's going to be a long, long dream, isn't it?" He lifted her hand and kissed it, then put it down in her lap again gently as if he feared a sudden movement might awaken them. "Perhaps it had better be at Mrs. Carnarvon's house—some morning just before luncheon and we could go quietly away afterward."

"Yes—and—tell me," she said, "wouldn't it be better for us not to go far away—and not to stay long? It seems to me that I most want to begin—begin our life together just as it will be."

"Are you afraid you wouldn't know what to do with me if I were idling about all day long?"

"Not exactly that. But I'd rather not take a vacation until we had earned it together."

"What a beautiful idea! I'll see what I can do."

They postponed the wedding until Howard had

the "art-department" of the *News-Record* well established. It was on a bright winter day in the second week of January that they stood up together and were married by the Mayor whom Howard had helped to elect. Only Mr. and Mrs. Carnarvon and Marian's brother were there. Then the six sat down to luncheon, and at three o'clock Howard and his wife started for Lakewood.

When they arrived a victoria was waiting. As soon as they were seated, Howard said "Home." The coachman touched his hat and the horses set out at a swift trot. The sun was setting and the dry, still air was saturated with the perfume of the snow-draped pines. Within five minutes the carriage was at a pretty little cottage with wide, glass-enclosed porches. They entered the hall. In the rooms on either side open fires were blazing an ecstatic welcome.

"How do you like 'home'?" asked Howard.

"I don't quite understand."

"You remember your plan of beginning at once. Well—this is the compromise. Stokely has let me have his house here for a month—we may keep it two if we like it. There is a telephone. The office isn't two hours away by rail. The newspapers are here early. We can combine work and play."

The manservant had left the room, a sort of library-reception room. Marian was seated in a big chair drawn near the fire. She had thrown back her wraps and was slowly drawing off her gloves. Howard stood at the side of the fire, leaning against the mantel and looking down at her.

"Before you definitely decide to stay—" he paused.

"Yes," she said, her colour heightening as she slowly lifted her eyes to his, "yes—why this solemn tone?"

"If ever—in the days that come—one never knows what may happen—if ever you should find that you had changed toward me——"

"Yes?"

"I ask you—don't promise—I never want you to promise me anything—I want you always—at every moment—to be perfectly free. So I just ask that you will let me see it. Then we can talk about it frankly, and we can decide what is best to do."

"But—suppose—you see I might still not wish to wound you—" she suggested, half teasing, half in earnest.

"It seems to me now that it is impossible that we can ever change. It seems to me—" he sat on the wide arm of her chair, and leaned over until his head touched hers, "that if you were to change it would break my heart. But if you were to change and were to hide it from me, I should find it out some day and——"

"And what——"

"It would be worse—a broken heart, a horror of myself, a—a contempt for you."

"Whatever comes, I'll be myself or try to be. Is that what you mean?"

"Exactly."

"And if you change?"

"But I shall not!"

"Why do you say that so positively?"

"Because—well, there are some things that we wish to believe and half believe, and some things that we believe that we believe, and some things that we *know*. I *know* about you—about my love for you."

"It is strange in a way, isn't it?" Marian was gently drawing her fingers through his. "This is all so different from what I used to think love would be. I used to picture to myself a man, something like you in appearance, only taller and fair, who would be my master, who would make me do what he wished. I think a woman always dreams of a lover who will be strong enough to be her ruler. And here——"

"So I am not the strong man that you look up to and tremble before? We shall see."

"Don't laugh at me. I mean that instead I have a man who makes me rule myself. You make me feel strong, not weak, and proud, not humble. You make me respect myself so."

"The democracy of love—freedom, equality, fraternity. Don't you like it?"

"Madame is served." It was the servant holding back one of the portières, his face expressionless, his eyes down.

* * * * * * * * *

Happiness evades description or analysis. We can only say that it reaches its highest point when a man and a woman, intelligent, appreciative, sympathetic, endowed with youth, health and freedom, are devoting their energies solely and determinedly to verifying each a preconceived idea of the other.

"And what do you think of it by this time?"

Marian asked the question in the pause after a twenty minutes' canter over a straightaway stretch through the pines.

"Of what?" Howard inquired. "I mean of what phase of it. Of you?"

"Well,—yes, of me—after a week."

"As I expected, only more so—more than I could have imagined. And you, what do you think?"

"It's very different from what I expected. It seemed to me beforehand that you, even you, would 'get on my nerves' just a little at times. I didn't expect you to appreciate—to feel my moods and to avoid doing—or is it that you simply cannot do—anything jarring. You have amazing instincts or else—" Marian looked at him and smiled mischievously, "or else you have been well educated. Oh, I don't mind—not in the least. No matter what the cause, I'm glad—glad—glad that you have been taught how to treat a woman."

"I see you are determined to destroy me," Howard was in jest, yet in earnest. "I am not used to being flattered. I have never had but one critic, and I have trained him to be severe and uncharitable. Now if you set me up on a high altar and wave the censors and cry 'glory, glory, glory,' I'll lose my head. You have a terrible responsibility. I trust you and I believe everything you say."

"I'll begin my duties as critic as soon as we go back to—to earth. But at present I'm going to be selfish. You see it makes me happier to blind myself to your faults."

They rode in silence for a few moments and then she said:

"I wish I had your feeling about—about democracy. I see your point of view but I can't take it. I know that you are right but I'm afraid my education is too strong for me. I don't believe in the people as you do. It's beautiful when you say it. I like to hear you. And I would not wish you to feel as I do I'd hate it if you did. It would be stooping, grovelling for you to make distinctions among people. But——"

"Oh, but I do make distinctions among people—so much so that I have never had a friend in my life until you came. I have been on intimate terms with many, but no one except you has been on intimate terms with me. Oh, yes, I'm one of the most exclusive persons in the world."

"That sounds like autocracy, doesn't it?" laughed Marian. "But you know I don't mean that. You think all the others are just as good as you are, only in different ways, whereas I feel that they're not. You don't mind vulgarity and underbreeding because you are perfectly indifferent to people so long as they don't try to jump the fence about your own little private enclosure."

"Oh, I believe in letting other people alone, and I insist upon being let alone myself. You see you make the whole world revolve about social distinctions. The fact is, isn't it, that social distinctions are mere trifles——"

"You oughtn't to waste time arguing with a prejudice. I admit that what I believe and feel is unreasonable. But I can't change an instinct. To me some people are better than others and are entitled to more, and ought to be looked up to and respected."

Howard had an answer on the tip of his tongue. His passion for high principle seemed to have been rekindled for the time by his love and in this tranquillising environment. He felt strongly tempted to reason with her unreasonableness, thus practically boasted as a virtue. It seemed so unworthy, this streak of snobbery, so senseless in an American at most three generations away from manual labour. But he had made up his mind long ago to trust to new surroundings, new interests to create in her a spirit more in sympathy with his career.

" She is too intelligent, too high-minded," he often reassured himself, " to cling to this stupidity of class-feeling. She has heard nothing but class-distinction all her life. Now that she is away from those people, with their petty routine of petty ideas, she will begin to see things as they are."

So he suppressed the argument and, instead, said in a tone of mock-pity: " Poor fallen queen—to marry beneath her. How she must have fought against the idea of such a plebeian partner."

" Plebeian—you ? " Marian looked at him proudly. " Why, one has only to see you to know."

" Yes, plebeian. I shall conceal it no longer. My ancestors were plain, ordinary, common, untitled Americans."

" Why, so were mine," she laughed.

" Don't ! You distress me. I should never have married you had I known that."

" I *am* absurd, am I not ? " Marian said gaily. " But

let me have my craze for well-mannered people and I'll leave you your craze for the—the masses."

They began to canter. Howard was smiling in spite of his irritation ; for it always irritated him to have her refuse to see his point in this matter—his distinction between a person as a friend and a person as a sociological unit.

He worked for an hour or two every morning and sometimes in the evening, Marian not far from his desk, so seated that when she turned the page of her book she could lift her eyes and look at him. She read the papers diligently every day for the first week. At the outset she thought she was interested. But she knew so little about newspaper details that she soon had to confess to herself that she was in fact interested in Howard as her husband and lover, and that his career interested her only in a broad, general way. What he talked about, that she understood and liked and was able to discuss. But the newspapers and the news direct suggested nothing to her, bored her.

"Just read that," he would say, pointing to an item. She would read it and wonder what he meant.

"It seems to me," she would think, "that it wouldn't in the least matter if that had not been printed." Then she would ask evasively but with an assumption of interest, "What are you going to do about it ?"

And he would explain the meaning between the lines ;

the hinted facts that ought to be brought out; the possibilities of getting a piece of news that would attract wide attention. And she would see it, sometimes clearly, usually vaguely; and she would admire him, but resume her unconquerable indifference to news.

She was soon looking at the paper only to read what he wrote; and she often thought how much more interesting he was as a talker than as a writer. "I'll start right when we get to town," she was constantly promising herself. "It must, must, must be *our* work."

Howard was, as she had told him, acutely sensitive to her moods. He did not formulate it to himself but simply obeyed an instinct which defined for him the limits of her interest. Before they had been at Lakewood a month, he was working alone without any expectation of sympathy or interest from her and without the slightest sense of loss in not getting it. Why should he miss that which he had never had, had never counted upon getting? He had always been mentally alone, most alone in the plans and actions bearing directly upon his own career. He was perfectly content to have her as the companion of his leisure.

Possibly, if he had been insistent, or if they had been in real sympathy instead of in only surface sympathy in most respects, she might have become interested in his work, might have impelled him to right development. But her distaste and inertia and his habit of debating and deciding questions as to the paper in his own mind, the fear of boring her, the dread of intruding upon her rights to her own individual tastes and feelings, restrained him without his having a sense of restraint.

When, after two months, they went up to town to stay, their course of life was settled, though Marian was protesting that it was not and Howard was unconscious of there having been any settlement, or anything to settle.

XXI.

WAVERING.

THEIR home was an apartment at Twenty-ninth Street and Madison Avenue—just large enough for two with its eleven rooms, all bearing the stamp of Marian's individuality. She had a keen sense of the beautiful and she had given her thought and most of her time between the early autumn and the wedding to making an attractive home. He had not seen her work until they came together in the late afternoon of a day in the last week of February.

"You—everywhere you," he said, as they inspected room after room. "I don't see how I could add anything to that. It is beautiful—the things you have brought together, I mean, the furniture, curtains, carpets, pictures, all beautiful in themselves, but——"

He was looking at her in that way which made her feel his great love for her even more deeply than when he put his arms about her and kissed her. "It reminds me of what I so often think about you. Nature gave you beauty but you make it wonderful because *you* shine through it, give it the force, the expression of your individuality. Other women have noses, eyes, chins, mouths as beautiful as yours. But only you produce such effects with the materials. I don't express it very well but—you understand?"

"Yes, I understand." She was leaning against him, her head resting upon his shoulder. "And you like your home?"

"We shall be happy here. I feel it in the air. This is a temple of the three great gods—Freedom, Love and Happiness. And—we'll keep the fires on the altars blazing, won't we?"

His hours were most irregular. Sometimes he was off to work early in the morning. Again he would not rise until noon. Sometimes he did not go to the office after dinner, and again he came hurriedly to dinner, not having the time to dress, and left immediately afterward to be gone until two, three or even four in the morning. At first Marian tried to follow his irregularities; but she was soon compelled to give up As he most often breakfasted about ten o'clock, she arranged to breakfast regularly at that hour. If he was not yet up, she waited about the house until she had seen him, listened while he talked of those "everlasting newspapers," praised his work a great deal, criticised it little and that gently. She made few and feeble struggles to interest herself in newspapers as newspapers. But he did not encourage her; other interests, domestic and social, clamoured for her time; and the idea of being directly useful to him in his work faded from her mind.

If she had loved him more sympathetically, if she had not been so super-sensitive to his passion for complete freedom, she would have resented what in another kind of man would have seemed frank neglect of her. But she thought she understood him and was deceived by his self-deceiving conviction that his work was her service and that the highest proof of his devotion to her was devotion to "our" career. Thus there was no bitterness or reproach of him, rarely much intensity, in her regret that they were together so little.

"Good morning, stranger!" she said, as he came into the dining room one day in early June.

He kissed her hand and then the "topknot" as he called the point into which her hair was gathered at the crown of her head. "It has been four days since I saw you," he said. And he sat opposite her looking at her with an expression of sadness which she had not seen since the first days of their acquaintance.

"I have missed you—you know," she was trying to look cheerful, "but I understand——"

"Yes," he interrupted. "You understand what I intend, understand that I mean my life to be for *us*. But sometimes—this morning—I think I am mistaken. It seems to me that I am letting this—" he threw his hand contemptuously toward the heap of morning newspapers beside him, "this trash comes between us. You are my real career, not these, and under the pretense of working for us I am spending my whole life, my one life, my one chance to help to make us happy, upon these." And he pushed the bundle of papers off the table.

"Something has depressed you." She was leaning her elbow upon the table and her chin upon her hand and was looking at him wistfully. "I wouldn't have you any different. You must follow the law of your nature. You must work at your ideal of being useful and influential in the world. You would not be satisfied to take my hand and trudge off with me through Arcadia to pick flowers and weave them into crowns for me. Nor should I," she laughed, "or I try to think I shouldn't."

"Let us go abroad for two months," he said. "I am tired, so tired. I am so weary of all these others, men and things."

"Can you spare the time?"

"I"—he corrected himself—"we have earned a vacation. It will be for me the first real vacation since I left Yale—thirteen years ago. I am growing narrow and stale. Let us get away and forget. Shall we?"

"The sooner the better—if this is not a passing mood. What has depressed you?" she persisted.

"What seems to be a piece of very good luck." He laughed almost sneeringly. "They have given me a share in the paper, twenty thousand in stock—which means a fixed income of five thousand a year so long as the paper pays what it does now—twenty-five per cent. And they offer me twenty thousand more at par to be paid for within two years. We are in a fair way to be rich."

"They don't want to lose you, evidently," she said. "But why does this make you sad? We are independent now—absolutely independent, both of us."

"Yes—we are rich. Together we have more than thirty-five thousand a year. But it is not what I wanted. I wanted to be free. Can a man be free who is rich, and rich in the way we are? Will my mind be open? Shall I dare to act and speak the truth? Or will our property, our environment, speak for me?"

"I can't imagine you a slave to mere dollars."

"Can't you? Well, I am afraid—I'm really afraid. I have always said that if I wished to enslave a people I would make them prosperous, would give them property, make them dependent upon their dollars. Then the fear of losing their dollars, their investments, would make them endure any oppression. Freedom's battles were never fought by men with full stomachs and full purses."

"But rich men have given up everything for freedom—Washington was a rich man."

"Ah, but how many Washingtons has the world produced? I see the time coming when I shall have to choose. I see it and—I dread it."

She rose and stood behind him leaning over with her arms about his neck and her cheek against his.

"You are brave. You are strong," she whispered. "You will meet that crisis if it comes and I have no fear, Mr. Valiant-for-Truth, as to how the battle will go."

He was glad that he did not have to face her eyes just then. "We will go abroad next Wednesday week," he whispered, "and we'll be happy in France—in Switzerland—in Holland—I want to see the park at the Hague again; and the tall trees with their straight big trunks green with moss; and the boughs meeting over the canals and making the clear water so black; and the snow-white swans sailing statelily about."

* * * * * * * * *

With the Atlantic between him and his work, he was able to suspend the habit of so many years. You would have fancied them just married, at whatever stage of their wanderings you might have met them. They were always laughing and talking—an endless flow of high spirits, absorption each in the other. They rose when they pleased, went to bed when it suited them. They had a manservant and a maid with them to relieve them of all the details. They travelled only in the afternoons, and then not far. If they missed one train, they cheerfully waited for another.

"I think we are achieving my ideal of vacation," he said.

"What is that—perfect idleness? We certainly are idle. I shouldn't have believed you could be so idle."

"Perfect idleness—yes. But more than that. I aimed far higher. My ideal was perfect irresponsibility. We have become like the wind that bloweth where it listeth."

And again, she said: "Let me see, what day is this?"

"I think it is Thursday or Friday," he replied. "But it may be Sunday. I can assure you that it is afternoon, late afternoon, and I think we ought to dress for dinner soon. After dinner, if you still care to know, and will remind me, I'll try to find out the day. But I'm sure we shall have forgotten before to-morrow."

Howard got an extension of his leave of absence and they roamed about England in August, reaching New York on the first day of September. Marian went on to Mrs. Carnarvon at Newport and Howard took rooms at the Waldorf. She stayed away a full week, then came to town, opened their apartment, and surprised him with a formal invitation to dinner.

He came like a guest and they went through all the formalities of meeting for the first time, of increasing intimacy—condensing a complete courtship into one evening.

"I thought you had had enough of me for the time," he said, as they sat in the wide window-seat, he tracing with his forefinger the line of the straps over her bare shoulders.

"And I thought that I would give you a chance to forget how nice I am and so give you the pleasure of learning all over again. But it was so lonely and miserable up there. 'Who can come after the king?'"

"Sometimes I think I ought to stir about more—meet the men who lead in the city. But it seems such a waste of time when I can come and call upon you."

"But might it not be better in the long run if you did meet these men? Mightn't it make your getting on quicker and easier?"

"Perhaps—if I were a gregarious animal, but I'm not. I'm shy and solitary and hard to get acquainted with. And it takes time to make friends. Besides, in making friends you also make enemies, and one enemy can do you more harm than all your friends can do you good. Then too, friends take up too much time. We have so little time and—we can spend it to so much better advantage—can't we?"

Marian pushed herself closer against him and presently said dreamily: "So much happiness, such utter happiness which no one, nothing can take away. I wonder when and how the first storm will come?"

"It needn't come at all—not for a long, long time. And when it does—we can weather it, don't you think?"

* * * * * * * * *

During the next two months they were together more than they had been in the spring. He imposed day office hours upon himself and did no work in the evenings except the correcting of editorial proofs which he had sent to him at the house, at the theatre, or at whatever restaurant they were dining. And at midnight he called up the office on the telephone and talked with Mr. King or Mr. Vroom about the news in hand and the programme for presenting it in the next morning's paper.

But as "people"—meaning Marian's friends—returned to town, they fell into the former routine. It was in part his doing, in part hers. He was now thirty-seven years old and his mind, always of a serious cast, was intolerant of trifles and triflers.

Marian's range of interests was shallower but much wider than his. Her beauty, her cleverness, her tact caused her to be sought. She invited many to their house and accepted more and more invitations. At first she never went without him. But he was sometimes compelled by his work to send her alone. He rarely went except for her sake—because he thought going about amused her. And he was glad and relieved when she began to go without him, instead of spending the evenings in solitude.

"There is no reason why you should punish yourself and punish me because you had the ill luck to marry a working-man," he said. "It cannot be agreeable to sit here all by yourself evening after evening. And it depresses me when I am at the office at night to think of you as lonely. It makes me happier in my work—my pleasure, you know—to think of you enjoying yourself."

"But aren't you afraid that some one will steal me?" she asked, laughingly.

"Not I." He was smiling proudly at her. "If you could be stolen, if you could be happier anywhere than with me, you have only to let me into the plot."

"There are some women who would not like that."

"And there are men who wouldn't feel as I do. But you and I, we belong to a class all by ourselves, don't we?"

Apparently they were as devoted each to the other as ever. But each now sought a separate happiness —he perforce in his work, she perforce in the only way left open to her. When they were together, which meant several hours every day and usually one whole day in the week, they were at once seemingly absorbed each in the other with all the rest as background. But none the less, they were leading separate lives, with separate interests, separate tastes, separate modes of thinking. The "bourgeois" life which they had planned—both standing behind the counter and both adding up the results of the day's business after they had put up the shutters, two as one in all the interests of life—became a dead and forgotten dream.

XXII.

THE SHENSTONE EPISODE.

ON the way to or from the opera or a party, she would peep in on him, watching the back of his head as he bent over his desk or read away at some dull-looking book, wishing that he would feel her presence and turn with that smile which was always hers from him, yet fearing to make a sound and compel his attention.

"At times I think," she said one day when he caught her in his arms on a sudden impulse and kissed her, "that the reason you don't try to rule me is because you don't care enough."

"That's precisely it." He was smoothing her eyebrows with his forefinger. "I don't care enough about ruling. I don't care enough for the sort of love that responds to 'must.'"

"But a woman likes to have 'must' said to her sometimes."

"Does she? Do you? Well—I'll say 'must' to you. You must love me freely and voluntarily, or not at all. You must do as you please."

"But don't you see that that drives me from you

often, keeps us apart in many ways. Now if you compelled me to think as you do, to like what you like——"

"But I couldn't. Then you would no longer be *you*. And I like you so well just as you are that I would not change an idea in your head."

Marian sighed and went away to her dinner party. She felt that she was in danger. "Not of falling in love with some other man," she thought, "for that's impossible. But if a man were to come along who invited me to be interested in his work, to keep him at whatever he was doing, I'd accept and that would lead on and on—where?"

She soon had an opportunity to answer that question. Howard went away to Washington to assist the party leaders in putting through a difficult tariff-reform bill which all the protected interests were fighting. He expected to be gone a week; but week after week passed and he was still at the capital, directing the paper by telegraph and sending Marian hurried notes postponing his return. She was going about daily, early and late, her life vacant, her mind restlessly seeking occupation, interest.

After he had been gone three weeks she found herself at dinner at Mrs. Provost's next to a tall, fair-haired athletic young man of about her own age. Something in his expression—perhaps the amused way in which he studied the faces of the others—attracted her to him. She glanced over at his card. It read "Mr. Shenstone."

"It doesn't add much to your information, does it?" he smiled, as he caught her glance rising from the card.

"Nothing," she confessed candidly. "I never heard of you before."

"And yet I've been splashing about, trying to attract attention to myself, for twelve years."

"Perhaps not in this particular pond."

"No, that is true."

"I was wondering what you do—lawyer, doctor, journalist, business man or what.

"And what did you conclude?"

"I concluded that you did nothing."

"You are right. But I try—I paint."

"Portraits?"

"Yes."

"That explains your way of looking at people. Only, you'll get no customers if you paint them as you see them."

"I only see what they see when they look in the mirror."

"Yes, but you see it impartially—or rather, I should say, cynically."

"Thank you."

"For what?"

"For calling me cynical. The two keenest pleasures a man can attain are for a woman to call him a cynic and for a woman to call him a devil with the women."

"Are you a 'devil with the women'?"

"Not I—not any more than I am a cynic. But let us talk about you—I am about exhausted as a topic of conversation. Why do you look so discontented?"

"Because I have nothing to occupy my mind."

"No children?"

"None—and no dogs."

"No husband?"

"Husbands are busy."

"So you are the typical American woman—the American instinct for doing, the universal woman's instinct for sunshine and laziness; the husband absorbed in his business or profession with his domestic life as an incident; the wife—like you."

"That is right, and wrong—nearer right than wrong, a little unjust to the husband."

"Oh, it's probably your fault that you are not absorbed in his business or profession. It ought to be as much yours as his. What does he do?"

"He edits a newspaper."

"Oh, he's *the* Mr. Howard. A very interesting, a very remarkable man."

Marian was delighted by this appreciation. She talked with Shenstone again after dinner and was pleased that he was to be in the same box with her at the opera the next night. He had spent much of his time on the other side of the Atlantic. He was unusually well educated for an artist's, and his mind was not developed in one direction only. Like Marian, his point of view was artistic and emotional. Like her he had a reverence for tradition, a deference to caste—the latter not offensive for the same reason that hers was not, because good birth and good breeding made him of the "high caste" and not a cringer with his eyes craned upward. It seemed in him, as in her, a sort of self-respect.

Marian showed a candid liking for his society and he was quick to take advantage of it. For a month they saw more and more each of the other, she discreet without deliberation and he discreet with deliberation. He talked to her of his work, of his ambition. He showed her himself without egotism. He made an impression upon her so distinct and so favourable that she admitted to herself that he was the most fascinating man—except one—whom she had ever met.

When Howard at last returned, defeated by corruption within his own party and for the time disgusted with politics, she at once had Shenstone at the house to dine. "What do you think of Mr. Shenstone?" she asked when they were alone.

"No wonder you're enthusiastic about him. As he talked to me, I could hardly keep from laughing. It was your own views, almost your own words. He has the look of a great man. I think he will 'arrive,' as they say in the Bowery."

Howard went out of his way to be agreeable to Shenstone, often inviting him to the house and giving him a commission to paint Marian. For the rest of the winter Shenstone was constantly in Marian's company, so constantly that they were gossiped about, and all the women who were unpleasantly discussed "for cause" conspired to throw them together as much as possible.

One evening in the very end of the winter, Howard called to Marian from his dressing room: "Why, lady, Shenstone's gone, hasn't he? I've just read a note from him."

There was a pause before Marian answered in a constrained voice: "Yes, he sailed to-day."

Howard was tying his bow. He paused at the curious tone, then smiled mysteriously to himself. He put on his waistcoat and coat and knocked on the half-open door. "May I come in?" he asked.

"Yes—I'm waiting for dinner to be announced."

She was sitting before the fire, very beautiful in her

evening gown. She seemed not to observe that he had entered but stared on into the flames. He stood beside her, looking down at her with the half mocking, half tender smile. Presently he sat upon the arm of her chair and took one of her hands. "Poor, friendless, beautiful lady," he said softly.

She glanced up quickly, her cheeks flaming but her eyes clear and frank. "Why do you say that?" she asked in the tone of one who knows why.

"Other women will not be her friends because they are jealous of her, and as for the men—how can a man be really a friend to a woman, a fascinating, sympathetic woman?"

Marian hid her face against the lapel of his coat. "He told me," she whispered, "and then he went away."

"He always does tell her. But——"

"But—what?"

"She doesn't always send him away. Poor fellow! Still, he went into it with his eyes open."

"He was very nice. He told it in a roundabout way. And I wasn't a bit afraid that he'd—he'd—you know. But I got to thinking about how I'd feel if he did—did touch me. And it made me—nervous."

There was a long pause, then she went on: "I wonder how you'd feel about touching another woman?"

"I? Dear me, I wonder! I never thought. You see I'm such a domestic, unattractive creature——"

"Don't laugh at me, please," she pleaded.

"I'm not laughing. Underneath, I'm thinking—thinking what I would do if I met you and lost you. It's very black on the Atlantic for one pair of eyes to-night."

"And the worst of it is," she said, "that my vanity is flattered and I'm not really sorry for him."

"Rather proud of her conquest, is she?"

"Yes, it pleased me to have him care."

"She likes to think that he'll carry his broken heart to the grave, does she?"

"Yes. Isn't it shameful?"

"Shameful? Shameless. I have always held that even the best woman dearly loves to ruin a man. It's such a triumph. And the more she loves him, the more she'd like to ruin him—that is, if ruin came solely through love for her and didn't involve her."

"But I would not want to ruin you."

"If that seemed to be the supreme test of my love for you—are you sure? I'm not. There's Thomas, knocking to announce dinner."

The Shenstone incident was apparently closed. Marian, a most attractive woman of thirty, absorbed in a social life that demanded all her physical and mental energy as well as all of her time, did not long vividly remember him. But he had given her a standard by which she unconsciously measured her husband. She contrasted the life he had promised her, the life Shenstone reminded her of, with the life that was—so material, so suspiciously physical when it professed to be loving, so suspiciously chill when it professed to be friendly. She thrust aside these thoughts as disloyal and false. But they persisted in returning.

If she had been less appreciative of Howard's intellect, less fascinated by the charm of his personality, she would soon have become one of the "misunderstood" women in search of "consolation." Instead, she turned her mind in the direction natural to her character—social ambition.

XXIII.

EXPANDING AND CONTRACTING.

IN such a city as New York, to be deliberately careful about money is the only way to keep within one's income, whether it be vast or small. There are temptations to buy at the end of every glance of the eye. The merchants are crafty in producing new and insidious allurements, in creating new and expensive tastes. But these might be resisted were it not that the habits of all one's associates are constantly and all but irresistibly stimulating the faculty of imitation.

Neither Howard nor Marian had been brought up to be watchful about money. Both had been accustomed to having their wants supplied. And now that they had a household and a growing income, it was a matter of course that their expenditures should steadily expand. Before three years had passed they were spending more than double the sum which at the outset they had fixed upon as their limit. A merely decent and self-respecting return of the hospitalities they accepted, a carriage and pair and two saddle horses and the servants to look after them—these items accounted for the increase. They looked upon this as really necessary expenditure and soon would have found that curtailment involved genuine deprivation. From the very beginning each step in expansion made the next logical and inevitable, made the plea of necessity seem valid.

An aunt of Marian's died, leaving her a "small" house—worth perhaps a quarter of a million—near the Avenue in Sixty-fifth Street, and eighty thousand in cash. About the same time Stokely told Howard of a fine speculative opportunity in certain copper properties. Howard hesitated. He knew that the way of speculation was the way of bondage for his newspaper and for him. But this particular adventure seemed harmless and he yielded. The money was invested and within a few months was producing an income of fifteen thousand a year which promised to be steady. Howard's ownership of stock in the paper increased; and as the profits advanced swiftly with its swift growth in its illustrated form, his own income was nearly fifty thousand a year. They were growing very rich. There was no longer the slightest anxiety as to money in his mind.

"You know the great dread I had in marrying," he said to her one day, "was lest I should make myself and you dependents, should some day sacrifice my freedom to my fear of losing—happiness."

"Yes, and very foolish you were, not to have more confidence in yourself and in me."

"Perhaps. But what I am thinking is that you have brought me luck. I am free, beyond anybody's reach. I could quit the paper to-morrow and we should hardly have to change our style of living even if I did not get something else to do."

"Style of living—" in that phrase lay the key to the change that was swiftly going on in Howard's mind and mental attitude. It is not easy for a man with environment wholly in his favour to keep his point of view correct, to keep his horizon wide and clear, his sense of proportion just. It is next to impossible for him to do so when his environment opposes.

The man who looks out from misery and squalor upon misery and squalor is, if he thinks at all, naturally an anarchist. To him the established order shows only injustice and persistence of injustice. The man who looks out from luxury and ease and well-being upon luxury and ease and well-being is forced by the very limitations of the human mind to an over-reverence for the established order. He is unreasonably suspicious of anything that threatens change. "When I'm comfortable all's well in the world; change might bring discomfort to me." And he flatters himself that he is a "conservative."

Howard had had a long training at the correct standpoint and in right thinking. But the influences were there, were at work, were destroying his devotion to a social and political ideal wholly alien to the life he was now living under the leading of his wife. He did not blame her, indeed he could not justly have blamed her, for his falling away from what he knew were correct principles for him. While she had brought him into this environment, while at first it was in large part for her that he gave so much time and thought to the accumulation of wealth, soon love of luxury, dependence upon a train of servants, fondness for the great extravagances to which New York tempts the rich and those living near the rich, became stronger in him than it was in her. And through the inevitable reaction of environment upon the man, the central point in his valuation of men and women tended to shift from the fundamentals, mind and character, to the surface qualities—dress and style and manners and refinement, and even dress.

This process of demoralisation was well advanced when they moved from the apartment. After four years of "expansion" there, they had begun to feel cramped; and a year after Marian inherited the house Howard had progressed to the mental, the moral, the financial state where it seemed natural, logical, practically necessary that they should set up a real New York "establishment."

"Isn't this just the house for us?" she said. "I hate huge, big houses. Like you, I think the taste of the occupants should be everywhere. Now this house is just big enough. You don't know how wonderful it would be."

"Oh, yes, I do," he laughed, "and you must try it." He was as enthusiastic as she.

In the late autumn the house was ready; and there was not a more artistic interior in New York. It was not so much the result of great expense as of intelligence and taste. It was an expression of an individuality—a revelation of a woman's beautiful mind, inspired by love.

"At last I have something to interest, to occupy me," she said. "This is our very own, through and through our own. It will be such a pleasure to me to keep it always like this."

"You—degenerated into a household drudge," he mocked. "Why, you used to laugh at me when I held up a wife who was a good housekeeper as one of my ideals."

"Did I?" she answered. "Well, as you would say, see what I've come to through living with—a member of the working-classes."

Howard's own particular part of this house included a library with a small study next to it. In the study was a most attractive table with plenty of room to spread about books and papers, a huge divan in the corner and a fire-place near by. He found himself doing more and more of his work at home. There were not so many interruptions as at the office, the beauty of the surroundings, the consciousness that "she" was not far away—all combined to keep him at home and to enable him to do more and better work there.

He was justly and greatly proud of her achievement; and where he used to be more regretful than he admitted even to himself when they had guests, he was now glad to see others about, admiring her taste, appreciating her skill as a hostess and giving him opportunities to look at her from an ever new point of view.

Of course these guests were almost all "*their* kind of people"—amiable, well mannered persons who thought and acted in that most conventional of moulds, the mould of "good society." They fitted into the surroundings, they did their part toward making those surroundings luxurious—a "wallow of self-complacent content." And this environment soon suited and fitted him exactly.

But to her he was still The Democrat. She loved him in the way and to the degree which her character, as the years had developed it, permitted her to love And this love, or rather admiring respect, was wholly based upon her ideal of him, her belief in the honesty and intensity of his convictions. While she did not share them, she had breadth enough to admire them and to regard them as high removed above her own ideas to which for herself she held tenaciously, instinct and association and "tradition" triumphing over reason.

Howard retained his ideal of her, never examining her closely, never seeing or suspecting what a pale love she gave him and how shrivelled had become the part of her nature which she and he both assumed was most strongly developed. He knew how she idealised him and did not dare to undeceive her. Therefore he practised toward her a hypocrisy that grew steadily more disgraceful, yet grew so gradually that there was no single moment at which he could conveniently halt and "straighten the record." At first he was often and heartily ashamed of himself; but by degrees this feeling deadened into cynical insensibility and he was only ashamed to let her see him as he really was. She had kept her self-respect. She esteemed self-respect at the exalted valuation he had formerly put upon it. What if she should find him out?

* * * * * * * * *

When the famous "coal conspiracy" was formed, three of the men conspicuous in it were among their intimates—that is, their families were often at his house and he and Marian were often at theirs. Yet he had never made a more relentless attack. Nor did he, either in the news columns or on the editorial page, conceal the connection of his three friends with the conspiracy.

"Mrs. Mercer was here this morning," Marian said as they were waiting for the butler to announce dinner. She was flushed and embarrassed.

Howard laughed. "And did she tell you what a dreadful husband you had?"

"Oh, she didn't blame you at all. She said they all knew how perfectly upright you were. Only, she said you did not understand and were doing Mr. Mercer a great injustice."

"Well, what do you think?"

"Why—I can't believe—is it possible, dear—I was just reading one of your editorials. Can Mr. Mercer be in such a scheme? The way she told it to me, he and the others were really doing a lot of people a valuable service, putting their property on a paying basis, enabling the railroads to meet their expenses and to keep thousands and thousands of men employed."

"Poor Mercer!" Howard said ironically. "Poor misunderstood philanthropist! What a pity that that sort of benevolence has to be carried on by bribing judges and prosecutors and legislatures, by making the poor shiver and freeze, by subtracting from the pleasures and adding to the anxieties of millions. One would almost say that such a philanthropy had better not be undertaken. It is so likely to be misunderstood by the 'unruly classes.'"

"Oh, I knew you were right. I told her you must be right, that you never wrote until you knew."

"And what was the result?"

"Well, we are making some very bitter enemies."

"I doubt it. I suspect that before long they'll come wheedling about in the hope that I'll let up on them or be a little easier next time."

"I'm sure I do not care what they do," said Marian, drawing herself up. "All I care for is—you, and to see you do your duty at whatever cost or regardless of cost—" she was leaning over the back of his chair with her arms about his neck and her lips very near to his ear—"you are my love without fear and without reproach."

"Listen, dear." He took her hand and drew her arms more closely about his neck. "Suppose that the lines were drawn—as they may be any day. Suppose that we had to choose, with all these friends of yours, with our position, yes, even the place I have won in my profession, my place as editor—all that we now have on the one side; and on the other side a thankless, unprofitable, apparently useless standing up for the right. Wouldn't you miss your friends?"

"*All* our friends? And who will be on the other side?"

"Almost no one that we know—that you would care to call upon or go about with or have here at the house. Nobody with any great amount of wealth or social position. Those other people who are in town when it is said 'Nobody is in town now!'"

She did not answer.

"Where would you be?" he repeated.

"Oh, I wasn't thinking of that." She came around and sat on his knee. "Where? Why, there's only one 'where' in all this world for me—'wheresoever thou goest.'"

And so the half-formed impulse to begin to straighten himself out with her was smothered by her.

Both were silent through dinner. She was thinking how honest, how fearless he was, how he loved her, how eagerly she would follow him, how blessed she was in the love of such a man. And he—he was regretting that his "pose" had carried him so far; he was wishing that he had not been so bitter in his attacks upon his and his wife's friends, the coal conspirators. When he had definitely cast in his lot with "the shearers" why persist in making his hypocrisy more abominable by protesting more loudly than ever in behalf of "the sheep?" Above all, why had he let his habit of voluble denunciation lead him into this hypocrisy with the woman he loved?

He admitted to himself that "causes" had ceased

to interest him except as they might contribute to the advancement of his power. Power !—that was his ambition now. First he had wished to have an independent income in order to be free. When he had achieved that, it was at the sacrifice of his mental freedom. And now, with the clearness of self-knowledge which only men of great ability have, he knew that the one cause for which he would make sacrifices was—himself.

"Of what are you thinking so gloomily?" she interrupted.

"Oh—I—let me see—well, I was thinking what a fraud I am; and that I wished I could dupe myself as completely as I can dupe——"

"Me?" she laughed. "Oh, we're all frauds—shocking frauds. I wouldn't have you see me as I really am for anything."

Although her remark was a commonplace, of small meaning, as he knew, he got comfort out of it, so desperately was he casting about for some consolation.

"That's true, my dear," he said. "And I wish that you liked the kind of a fraud I am as well as I like the kind of a fraud you are."

XXIV.

"MR. VALIANT-FOR-TRUTH."

STOKELY came rushing into his office the next morning. "Good God, old man," he exclaimed, "What's the meaning of this attack on the coal roads?"

Howard flushed with resentment, not at what Stokely said, but at his tone.

"Now, don't get on your high horse. I don't think you understand." Stokely's tone had moderated. "Don't you know that the Delaware Valley road is in this?"

Howard started. He had just invested two hundred thousand dollars in that stock on Stokely's advice "No, I didn't know it." He recovered himself. "And furthermore I don't give a damn." He struck his desk angrily. His simulation of incorruptible indignation for the moment half deceived himself.

"Why, man, if this infernal roast is kept up, you'll lose a hundred thousand. Then there are my interests. I'm up to my neck in this deal."

"My advice to you is to get out of it. I'm sorry, but you know as well as I do that the thing is infamous."

"Infamous—nonsense! It will double our dividends and the consumers won't feel it."

"Let us not discuss it, Stokely. There—don't say anything you'll regret."

"But——"

"Now, Stokely—don't argue it with me."

Stokely put on his hat, stood up and looked at Howard with sullen admiration. "You will drive away the last friend you've got on earth, if you keep this up. Good morning."

Howard sent a smile of cynical amusement after him, then stared thoughtfully into the mass of papers on his desk for five, ten, fifteen minutes. When his plan was formed he touched the electric button.

"Please tell Mr. King I'd like to see him," he said to the answering boy.

Mr. King entered with a bundle of legal documents. "I suppose it's the injunction you want to discuss," he said. "We've got the papers all ready. It's simply great. Those fellows will be in a corner and will have to give up. They can't get away from us. The price of coal will drop half a dollar within a week, I'll bet."

"I'm afraid you are over sanguine," Howard said. "I've just been going over the matter with my lawyer. But leave the papers with me. And—about the news—be careful what you say. We've been going a little strong. I think a little less personal matter would be advisable."

Mr. King was amazed and looked it. He slowly pulled himself together to say, "All right, Mr. Howard. I think I understand." He laid the papers down and departed. Outside the door he laughed softly to himself. "Somebody's been cutting his comb, I guess," he murmured. "Well, I didn't think he'd last. New York always gets 'em when they're worth while."

As the door closed behind King, Howard drew out the lowest and deepest drawer of his desk. It was half-filled with long-undisturbed pamphlets and newspaper cuttings. He tossed in the injunction papers. A cloud of dust flew up and settled thickly upon them. He shut the drawer.

He went to the window and looked out over the city—that seductive, that overwhelming expression of wealth and power. "What was it my father wrote me when I told him I was going to New York?" and he recalled almost the exact words—"New York that lures young men from the towns and the farms, and prostitutes them, teaches them to sell themselves with unblushing cheeks for a fee, for an office, for riches, for power." He shrugged his shoulders, smiled, drew himself up, returned to his desk and was soon absorbed in his work.

The next morning the *News-Record's* double-leaded

"leader" on the Coal Trust was a discharge of heavy artillery. But it was artillery in retreat. And in the succeeding days, the retreat continued—not precipitate but orderly, masterly.

* * * * * * * * *

Ten days after their talk on the "coal conspiracy" Marian greeted him late in the afternoon with "Oh, such a row with Mrs. Mercer!"

"Mrs. Mercer! Why, what was she angry about?"

"She wasn't—at least, not at first. It was I. I went to see her and she asked me to thank you for stopping that fight on the coal conspiracy."

"That was tactful of her," Howard said, turning away to hide his nervousness.

"And I told her that you had not stopped, that you wouldn't stop until you had broken it up. And she smiled in a superior way and said I was quite mistaken, that I didn't read the paper. I haven't read it for several days, but I knew *you*, dear, and I remembered what you had said. And so we just had it. We were polite but furious when I went. I shall never go near her again."

"But, unfortunately, we have stopped. We had to do it. We could accomplish nothing."

"Oh, it doesn't matter. What angered me was her insinuation."

"That was irritating. But, tell me, what if it had

been true?" Howard's voice was strained and he was looking at her eagerly, with fever in his eyes.

"But it couldn't be. It isn't worth while imagining. You could not be a coward and a traitor." So complete was her confidence in him that suspicion of him was impossible.

"Would you sit in judgment on me?"

"Not if I could help it."

"But you can—you could help it." His manner was agitated, and he spoke almost fiercely. "I am free," he went on, and as she watched his eyes she understood why men feared him. "I do what I will. I am not accountable to you, not even to you. I have never asked you to approve of me, to approve what I do, to love me. You are free also, free to love, free to withdraw your love. I follow the law of my own being. You must take me as you find me or not at all."

She tried to stop him but could not. His words poured on. He leaned forward and took her hand and his eyes were brilliant and piercing. "I love you," he said. "Ah, how I love you—not because you love me, not because you are an angel, not because you are a superior being. No, not for any reason in all this wide world but because you are you. Do what you will and I shall love you. Whether I had to look up among the stars or down in the mire to find you, I would look just as steadily, just as proudly."

He drew a long breath and his hand trembled. "If I were a traitor, then, if you loved me, you would say, 'What! Is he to be found among traitors? How I love treason!' If I were a coward, liar, thief, a sum of all the vices, then, if you ever had loved me you would love me still. I want no love with mental reservations, no love with ifs and buts and provided-thats. I want love, free and fearless, that adapts itself to changing human nature as the colour of the sea adapts itself to the colour of the sky; love that does not have to be cajoled and persuaded lest it be not there when I most need it. I want the love that loves."

"You know you have it." She had been compelled by his mood and was herself in a fever. She looked at him with the expression which used to make his nerves vibrate. "You know that no human being ever was more to another than I to you. But you can't expect me to be just the same as you are. I love *you*—not the false, base creature you picture. I admire the way you love, but I could not love in that way. Thank God, my love, my dear—I shall never be put to that test. For my love for you is my—my all."

"We are very serious about a mere supposition."

Howard was laughing, but not naturally. "We take each the other far too seriously. I'm sorry you idealise me so. Who knows—you might find me out some day—and then—well, don't blame me."

Marian said no more, but late that evening she put her hands on his shoulders and said: "You're not hiding something from me—something we ought to bear together?"

"Not I." Howard smiled down into her eyes and kissed her.

His mood of reaction, of hysteria had passed. He was thinking how little in reality she had had to do with his outburst. He had not been addressing her at all, except as she seemed to him for the moment the embodiment of his self-respect—or rather, of an "absurd," "extremely youthful" ideal of self-respect which he had "outgrown."

XXV.

THE PROMISED LAND.

A WOMAN with a powerful personality may absorb in herself a man of strong and resolute ambition, may compel him to make her his career, to feel that to get and to keep her is all that he asks from destiny. But Marian was not such a woman.

She had come into Howard's life at just the time and in just the way to arouse his latent passion for power and to give it a sufficient initial impetus. It was love for her that set him to lifting himself from among those who work through themselves alone to the potent few who work chiefly by directing the labour of others.

Once in this class, once having tasted the joy of power, Howard was lost to her. She was unable to restrain or direct, or even clearly to understand. She became an incident in his life. As riches came with power, they pushed him to one side in her life. Living in separate parts of a large house, leading separate lives, rarely meeting except when others were present —following the typical life of New Yorkers of fortune and fashion—they gradually grew to know little and see little and think little each of the other.

There was no abruptness in the transition. Every day had contributed its little toward widening the gap. There was no coolness, no consciousness of separation; simply the slow formation of the habit of complete independence each of the other.

His ambitions absorbed his thought and his time. To them he found her very useful. The social side —forming and keeping up friendly relations with the families whose heads were men of influence—was a vital part of his plan. But he used her just as he used every and any one else whom he found capable of contributing to his advancement; and, as she never insisted upon herself, never sought to influence or even to inquire into his course of action, she did not find him out.

She was in a vague way an unhappy woman. A discontent, a feeling that her life was incomplete, perpetually teased her. He was distinctly unhappy, often gloomy, at times morose. In her rare analytic moods she attributed their failure to prolong the happiness of their courtship to the hard work which kept him from her, kept them from enjoying the great love which she assumed they felt each for the other. She would not and could not see that that love had long disappeared, leaving a mask of forms, of phrases and of impulses of passion to conceal its departure. And to this view he outwardly assented, when she suggested it;

but he knew that she was deceiving herself as to him, and wondered if she were not deceiving herself as to her own feelings.

Up to the time of the "Coal Conspiracy" and his attempt to put himself straight with her, the idea of his love for her and of her oneness with him had at least a hold upon his imagination. He then saw how far apart they had drifted; and he dismissed from his mind even the pretense that love played any part in his life. After that definite break with principle and self-respect for the sake of his coal holdings, his Wall Street friends and his newspaper career, the development of his character continued along strictly logical lines with accelerating speed. And it was accompanied by an ever franker, more cynical acceptance of the change.

He could not deceive himself, nor can any man with the clearness of judgment necessary to great achievement—although many "successful" men, for obvious reasons of self-interest, diligently encourage the popular theory of warped conscience. He was well aware that he had shifted from the ideal of use *to* his fellow-beings to the ideal of use *of* his fellow-beings, from the ideal of character to the ideal of reputation. And he knew that the two ideals can not be combined and that he not only was not attempting to combine them but had no desire so to do. He despised his former ideals; but also he despised himself for despising them.

His quarrel with himself was that he seemed to himself a rather vulgar sort of hypocrite. This was highly disagreeable to him, as his whole nature tended to make him wish to be himself, to make him shrink from the part of the truckler and the sycophant which he was playing so haughtily and so artistically. At times it exasperated him that he could not regard his change of front as a deliberate sale for value received, and not as the weak and cowardly surrender which he saw that it really was.

* * * * * * * * *

On the day after Howard's forty-fourth birthday Coulter fell dead at the entrance to the Union Club. When Stokely heard of it he went direct to the *News-Record* office.

"I happen to know something about Coulter's will," he said to Howard. "The *News-Record* stock is to be sold and you and I are to have the first chance to take it at three hundred and fifty—which is certainly cheap enough."

"Why did he arrange to dispose of the most valuable part of his estate?"

"Well, we had an agreement about it. Then, too, Coulter had no faith in newspapers as a permanent investment. You know there are only the widow, the girl and that worthless boy. Heavens, what an ass that boy is! Coulter has tied up his estate until the youngest grandchild comes of age. He hopes that there will be a son among the grandchildren who will realise his dream."

"Dream?" Howard smiled. "I didn't know that Coulter ever indulged in dreams."

"Yes, he had the rich man's mania—the craze for founding a family. So everything is to be put into real estate and long-term bonds. And for years New York is to be reminded of Samuel Coulter by some incapable who'll use his name and his money to advertise nature's contempt for family pride in her distributions of brains. I think even a fine tomb is a wiser memorial."

"Well, how much of the stock shall you take?" Howard asked.

"Not a share," Stokely replied dejectedly. "Coulter couldn't have died at a worse time for me. I'm tied in every direction and shall be for a year at least. So you've got a chance to become controlling owner."

"I?" Howard laughed. "Where could I get a million and a half?"

"How much could you take in cash?"

"Well—let me see—perhaps—five hundred thousand."

"You can borrow the million with the stock as collateral."

"But how could I pay?"

"Why, your dividends at our present rate would be more than two hundred thousand a year. Your interest charge would be under seventy-five thousand. Perhaps I can arrange it so that it won't be more than fifty thousand. You can let the balance go on reducing the loan. Then I may be able to put you onto a few good things. At any rate you can't lose anything. Your stock would bring five hundred even at forced sale. It's your chance, old man. I want to see you take it."

"I'll think it over. I have no head for figures."

"Let me manage it for you." Stokely rose to go. Howard began thanking him, but he cut him off with:

"You owe me no thanks. You've made money for me—big money. I owe you my help. Besides, I don't want any outsider in here. Let me know when you're ready." He nodded and was gone.

"What a chance!" Howard repeated again and again.

He was looking out over New York.

Twenty years before he had faced it, asking of it nothing but a living and his freedom. For twenty years he had fought. Year by year, even when he seemed to be standing still or going backward, he had steadily gained, making each step won a vantage-ground for forward attack. And now—victory. Power, wealth, fame, all his!

Yet a deep melancholy came over him. And he fell to despising himself for the kind of exultation that filled him, its selfishness, its sordidness, the absence of all high enthusiasm. Why was he denied the happiness of self-deception? Why could he not forget the means, blot it out, now that the end was attained?

His mind went out, not to Marian, but to that other—the one sleeping under the many, many layers of autumn leaves at Asheville. And he heard a voice saying so faintly, so timidly: "I lay awake night after night listening to your breathing, and whispering under my breath, 'I love you, I love you. Why can't you love me?'" And then—he flung down the cover of his desk and rushed away home.

"Why did I think of Alice?" he asked himself. And the answer came—because in those days, in the days of his youth, he had had beliefs, high principles; he had been incapable of this slavery to appearances, to vain show, incapable of this passion for reputation regardless of character. His weaknesses were then weaknesses only, and not, as now, the laws of his being controlling his every act.

He smiled cynically at the self of such a few years ago—yet he could not meet those honest, fearless eyes that looked out at him from the mirror of memory.

He was triumphant, but self-respect had gone and not all the thick swathings of vanity covered him from the stabs of self-contempt.

"When I am really free, when the paper is paid for and I can do as I please, why not try to be a man again? Why not? It would cost me nothing."

But a man is the sum of *all* his past.

XXVI.

IN POSSESSION.

STOKELY arranged the loan, and within six months Howard was controlling owner of the *News-Record.* There was a debt of a million and a quarter attached to his ownership, but he saw how that would be wiped out. Once more he threw himself into his work with the energy of a boy. He had to give much of his time to the business department—to the details of circulation and advertising. He felt that the profits of the paper could be greatly increased by improving its facilities for reaching the advertiser and the public. He had never been satisfied with the circulation methods; but theretofore his ignorance of business and his position as mere salaried editor had acted in restraint upon his interference with the "ground floor."

As he had suspected, the business office was afflicted with the twin diseases—routine and imitativeness. It followed an old system, devised in days of small circulation and grudgingly improved, not by thought on the part of those who circulated the paper, but by compulsion on the part of the public. No attempts were made to originate schemes for advertising the paper. The only methods were wooden variations upon placards in the street cars and the elevated stations, and cards hung up at the news-stands. As for getting advertising business, they thought they showed enterprise by a little canvassing among the conspicuous merchants in Greater New York.

Howard had charts made showing the circulation by districts. With these as a basis he ordered an elaborate campaign to " push " the paper in the districts where it was circulated least and to increase its hold where it was strong. " We do not reach one-third of the people who would like to take our paper," he told Jowett, the business manager. " Let us have an army of agents and let us take up our territory by districts."

The Sunday edition was the largest source of revenue, both because it carried a great deal more advertising at much higher rates than did the week-day editions, and because it sold at a price which yielded a profit on the paper itself, while the price of the week-day editions did not. News constituted less than one-fourth of its contents. The rest was " feature articles," as interesting a week late to a man in Seattle as on the day of publication within a mile of the office.

" We get out the very best magazine in the market," said Howard to Jowett. " Are we pushing it in the east, in the west, in the south? Look at the charts.

We have a Sunday circulation of five hundred in Oregon, of one thousand in Texas, of six hundred in Georgia, of two thousand in Maine. Why not ten times as much in each of those states? Why not ten times as much as we now have near New York?"

There was no reason except failure to "push" the paper. That reason Howard proceeded to remove. But these enterprises involved large expenditures, perhaps might mean postponement of the payment of the debt. Receipts must be increased and the most promising way was an increase in the advertising business.

Howard noted on the chart nineteen cities and large towns near New York in each of which the daily circulation of the *News-Record* was equal to that of any paper published there and far exceeded the combined circulations of all the home dailies on Sunday. This suggested a system of local advertising pages, and for its working out he engaged one of the most capable newspaper advertising men in the city. Within three months the idea had "caught on" and, instead of sending useless columns of New York "want-ads" and the like to places where they could not be useful, the *News-Record* was presenting to its readers in twelve cities and towns the advertisements of their local merchants.

A year of this work, with Howard giving many

hours of each day personally to tiresome details, brought the natural results. The profits of the *News-Record* had risen to five hundred and forty thousand, of which Howard's share was nearly three hundred thousand. The next year the profits were seven hundred and fifty thousand, and Howard had reduced his debt to eight hundred thousand.

"We shall be free and clear in less than three years," he said to Marian.

"If we have luck," she added.

"No—if we work—and we shall. Luck is a stone which envy flings at success."

"Then you don't think you have been lucky?"

"Indeed I do not."

"Not even," she smiled, drawing herself up.

"Not even—" he said with a faint, sad answering smile. "If you only knew how hard I worked preparing myself to be able to get you when you came; if you only, only knew how life made me pay, pay, pay; if you only knew——"

"Go on," she said, coming closer to him.

He sighed—not for the reason of sentiment which she fancied, though he put his arms around her. "How willingly I paid," he evaded.

He went to his desk and she stood looking at him. There was still the charm of youth, even freshness, in her beauty—and she was not unconscious of the fact.

And he—he was handsome, distinguished looking and certainly did not suggest age or the approach of age; but in his hair, so grey at the temples, in the stern, rather haughty lines of his features, in the weariness of his eyes, there was not a vestige of youth. "How he has worked for me and for his ideals," she thought, sadly yet proudly. "Ah, he is indeed a great man, and *my* husband!" And she bent over him and kissed him on an impulse to a kind of tenderness which was now so strange to her that it made her feel shy.

"And what a radical you'll be," she laughed, after a moment's silence. "What a radical, what a democrat!"

"When?" He was flushing a little and avoided her eyes.

"When you're free—really the proprietor—able to express your own views, all your own views. We shall become outcasts."

"I wonder," he replied slowly, "does a rich man own his property or does it own him?"

For an instant he had an impulse of his old longing for sympathy, for companionship. She was now thirty-six and, save for an expression of experience, of self-control, seemed hardly so much as thirty. But with the years, with the habit of self-restraint, with instinctive rather than conscious realisation of his indifference toward her, had come a chill perceptible at the surface and permeating her entire character. In her own way she had become as self-absorbed, as ambitious as he.

He looked at her, felt this chill, sighed, smiled at himself. Yes, he was alone—and he preferred to be alone.

XXVII.

THE HARVEST.

THROUGH all his scheming and shifting Howard had kept the *News-Record* in the main an "organ of the people." Coulter and Stokely had on many occasions tried to persuade him to change, but he had stood out. He did not confess to them that his real reason was not his alleged principles but his cold judgment that the increases in circulation which produced increases in advertising patronage were dependent upon the paper's reputation of fearless democracy.

In the fourth year of his ownership he felt that the time had come for the change, that he could safely slip over to the other side—the side of wealth and power, the winning side, the side with offices and privileges to distribute. His debt was so far reduced that he had nothing to fear from it. A presidential campaign was coming on and was causing unusual confusion, a general shift of party lines. And he had put the *News-Record* in such a position that it could move in any direction without shock to its readers.

The "great battle" was on—the battle he had in his younger days looked forward to and longed for—

the battle against Privilege and for a "restoration of government by the people." The candidates were nominated, the platforms put forward and the issue squarely joined.

The same issue had been involved in previous campaigns; but the statement of the case by the party opposed to "government of, by and for plutocracy" had been fantastic, extreme, entangled with social, economic and political lunacies. And Howard had strengthened the *News-Record* by refusing to permit it to "go crazy." Now, however, there was in honesty no reason for refusing support to the advocates of his professed principles.

But the *News-Record* was silent. Howard and Marian went away to their cottage at Newport, and he left rigid instructions that no political editorials were to be published except those which he might send. There he got typhoid fever and was at the point of death for two weeks.

Marian gave herself to nursing him, stayed close beside him, read books and the newspapers to him throughout his convalescence. They were more intimate than they had been for years. A feeling bearing a remote resemblance to the love he had once had for her arose out of his weakness and dependence and his seclusion from the instruments and objects of his ambition. And she swept aside the barriers she had erected between herself and him and returned, as nearly as one may, to the love and interest of their early days together.

In the first week of September came Stokely with Senator Hereford, the chairman of the "Plutocracy" campaign committee.

"I shall not annoy you with evasions," said Hereford, "as Mr. Stokely assures me that I may speak freely to you, that you personally are with us. The fact is, our campaign is in a bad way, especially in New York State, and there especially in New York City."

"You surprise me," said Howard. "All my information has come from the newspapers which my wife reads me. I had gathered that the victory was all but won."

"We encourage that impression. You know how many weak-kneed fellows there are who like to be on the winning side. We've been pouring out the money and stand ready to pour it out like water. But these damned reform ballot-laws make it hard for us to control the vote. We buy, but we fear that the goods will not be delivered. Feeling is high against us. Even our farmers and shopkeepers are acting queerly. And the other fellows have at last put up a safe man on a conservative platform."

Howard turned his face away. There was still the

memory, the now quickened memory, of his former self to make him wince at being included in such an "us."

"You can't afford to keep silent any longer," Hereford continued. "You've done the cause a world of good by your silence thus far. You have the reputation of being the leading popular organ, and your keeping quiet has meant thousands of votes for us. But the time has come to attack. And you must attack if we are to carry New York. You can turn the tide in the state, and—well, we have a very high regard for your genius for making your points clearly and interestingly. We need your ideas for our editors and speakers as much as we need your influence."

"I cannot discuss it to-day," Howard answered after a moment's silence. "It would be a grave step for the *News-Record* to take. I am not well, as you see. To-morrow or next day I'll decide. You'll see my answer in the paper, I think." He closed his eyes with significant weariness.

Hereford looked at him uneasily. Just outside the door Stokely whispered, "Don't be alarmed. You've got him. He's with us, I tell you."

"I must make sure," whispered Hereford. "I wish to speak to him alone for a moment."

"I beg your pardon, Mr. Howard," he said as he re-entered the room. "I forgot an important part of my mission. Our candidate authorized me to say to you on his behalf that he felt sure you would see your duty; that he esteemed your character and judgment too highly to have any doubts; and that he intends to show his appreciation of the conscientious, independent vote which is rallying to his support; in the event of his election, he feels that he could not do so in a more satisfactory manner than by offering you either a place in his cabinet or an ambassadorship as you may prefer."

As soon as Howard saw Hereford returning, he knew the reason. He had never before been offered a bribe; but he could not mistake the meaning of Hereford's bold yet frightened expression. He kept his eyes averted during the delivery of the long, rambling sentence. At the end, he looked at Hereford frankly and said in his most gracious manner:

"Thank him for me, will you? And express my appreciation of so high a compliment from such a man."

Hereford looked relieved, delighted. "I'm glad to have met you, Mr. Howard, and to have had so satisfactory an interview."

Again outside the door, he muttered gleefully: "Yes, we've   him. Otherwise he would have had his servants kick me down stairs. Gad, no wonder —— is on his way to the Presidency. I had a sneaking fear that this fellow might be sincere. But *he* saw through him without ever having seen him. I suppose two men of that stripe instinctively understand each other."

* * * * * * * * *

That was on a Sunday afternoon. On the following Wednesday, as Marian came into Howard's sitting-room with the newspapers, she laughed: "I've been reading such a speech from your candidate, you radical! I must say I liked to read it. It was so like you, your very phrases in many places, the things you used to talk to me before you gave me up as hopeless. Just listen."

And she read him the oration—a reproduction of the Howard she first saw, the Howard she admired and loved and had never lost. "Isn't it superb?" she asked at the end. "You must have written it for him. Don't you like it?"

"Very able," was Howard's only comment.

Marian continued to read the paper, glancing from column to column, giving him the substance of the news. Soon she reached the editorial page. He was stealthily watching her face. He saw her glance through a few lines of the leader, start, read on, look in a terrified way at him, and then skip abruptly to the next page.

"Read me the leader, won't you?" he asked.

"My voice is tired," she pleaded. "I'll read it after awhile."

"Please," he insisted. "I'm especially anxious to hear it."

"I think," she almost stammered, "that somebody has taken advantage of your illness. I didn't want to tell you until I'd had a chance to think."

"Please read it." His tone was abrupt. She had never heard that tone before.

She read. It was an assertion of that which *her* Howard most disbelieved, most protested against; a defense of the public corruption she had heard him denounce so often; an attack upon the ideas, the principles, the elements she had so often heard him eulogize. It was as adroit as it was detestable, as plausible as it was unprincipled.

When she had done, there was a long silence which he broke. "What do you think of it?"

"Only a wretch, an enemy of yours could have written it. Who can it have been?" Her eyes were ablaze and her voice trembled with anger.

"I wrote it," he said.

He did not dare to look at her for a few seconds. Then, with a flimsy mask of pretended calmness only the more clearly revealing self-contempt and cowardice, he faced her amazed eyes, her pale cheeks, her parted lips—and dropped his gaze to the floor.

"You?" she whispered. "You?"

"Yes, I."

She sat so still that he reached over and touched her hand. It was cold. She shivered and drew it away. They were silent for a long time—several minutes. She was looking at his face. It was old and sad and feeble—pitiful, contemptible. She had never seen those lines of weakness about his mouth before. She had never before noted that his features had lost the expression of exalted character, the light of free and independent manhood which made her look again the first time she saw him. When had the man she loved departed? When had the new man come? How long had she been giving herself to a stranger—and *such* a stranger?

"Yes—I," he repeated. "I have come over to your side." He laughed and she shivered again. "Well—what do you think?"

"Think?—I?—Oh, I think——"

She burst into tears, flung herself down at his feet and buried her head in his lap.

"I think nothing," she sobbed, "except that I—I love you."

He fell to smoothing her hair, slowly, gently, patronisingly. His face was composed and he was looking down at her trembling head and agitated shoulders with an absent-minded smile. How easily this once dreaded crisis had passed! How he had overestimated her! How he had underestimated himself!

His glance and his thoughts soon fastened upon the copy of his newspaper which she had thrown aside—*his* newspaper indeed, his creation and his creature, the epitome of his intellect and character, of his strength and his weakness. Half a million circulation daily, three quarters of a million on Sunday—how mighty as a direct influence upon the people! Its clearness and vigour, its intelligence, its truth-like sophistry—how mighty as an indirect influence upon the minds of other editors and of public men! "Power—Success," he repeated to himself in an exaltation of vanity and arrogance.

Marian lifted her head and, turning, put it against his knee. She reached out for his hand. He began to speak at once in a low persuasive voice:

"Trust me, dear, can't you? You do not—have not been reading the paper until recently. You are not interested in politics. There have been many changes in the few last years. And I too have changed. I am no longer without responsibilities. They have sobered me, have given me an appreciation of property, stability, conservatism. Youth is enthusiastic, theoretical. I have——"

"Ah, but I do trust you," she interrupted eagerly,

fearful lest his explanations would make it the more difficult for her to convince herself of what she felt she must believe if life were to go on. "And you—I don't want you to excite yourself. You must be quiet —must get well."

Each avoided meeting the other's eyes as she arranged the pillows for him before leaving him alone to rest.

The longer she juggled with her discovery the less appalling it seemed. His line of action fitted too closely to her own ambitions of social distinction, social leadership. If he had been her lover, the shock would have killed love and set up contempt in its stead. But he was not her lover, had not been for years; and to find that her husband was doing a husband's duty, was winning position and power for himself and therefore for his wife—that was a disclosure with mitigating aspects at least. Besides, might she not be in part mistaken? Surely any course so satisfactory in its results could not be wholly wrong, might perhaps be the right in an unexpected, unaccustomed form.

XXVIII.

SUCCESS.

FRENCH had made a portrait of the new American ambassador to the Court of St. James and it was shown at the spring exhibition of the Royal Academy. The ambassador and his wife wished to see how it had been hung, but they did not wish to be seen. So they chose an early hour of a chill, rainy May morning to drive in a hansom from their place in Park Lane to Burlington House.

They found the portrait in Room VI, on the line, in a corner, but where it had the benefit of such light as there was. When they entered no one was there; but, as they were standing close to the picture, admiring the energy and simplicity of the strokes of the master's brush, a crowd swept in and enclosed them.

"Let us go," Howard said in a low tone.

Just then a man, almost at his shoulder because of the pressure of those behind, said: "Wonderful, isn't it? I've never seen a better example of his work. He had a subject that suited him perfectly."

"No, let us stay," Marian whispered in reply to her

husband. " They can't see our faces and I'd like to hear."

"Yes, it is superb," came the answer to the man behind them in a voice unmistakably American. " Now, tell me, Saverhill, what sort of a person would you say the ambassador is from that picture? You don't know him?"

" Never heard of him until I read of his appointment," replied the first voice.

" I've heard of him often enough," came in the American voice. " But I've never seen him."

"You know him now," resumed the Englishman, " inside as well as out. French always paints what he sees and always sees what he's painting."

" Well, what is it?"

" Let us go," whispered Marian. But Howard did not heed her.

" I see—a fallen man. He was evidently a real man once; but he sold himself."

" Yes? Where does it show?"

" He's got a good mind, this fellow-countryman of yours. There are the eyes of a thinker and a doer. Nothing could have kept him down. His face is almost as relentless as Kitchener's and fully as aggressive, except that it shows intellect, and Kitchener's doesn't. Now note the corners of his eyes, Marshall, and his mouth and nostrils and chin, and you'll see why he sold himself, and the—the consequences."

Howard and Marian, fascinated, compelled, looked where the unknown requested.

"I think I see what you mean," came in Marshall's voice, laughingly. "But go on."

"Ah, there it all is—hypocrisy, vanity, lack of principle, and, plainest of all, weakness. It's a common enough type among your successful men. The man himself is the fixed market price for a certain kind of success. But, according to French, this ambassador of yours seems to know what he has paid; and the knowledge doesn't make him more content with his bargain. He has more brains than vanity; therefore he's an unhappy hypocrite instead of a happy self-deceiver."

Howard and Marian shrunk together with their heads close in the effort to make sure of concealing their faces. She was suffering for herself, but more acutely for him. She knew, as if she were looking into his mind, his frightful humiliation. "Hereafter," she thought, "whenever any one looks at him he will feel the thought behind the look."

"How nearly did I come to him?" asked Saverhill.

Howard started and Marian caught the rail for support.

"A centre-shot," replied Marshall, "if the people who know him and have talked to me about him tell the truth."

"Oh, they're 'on to' him, as you say, over there, are they?"

"No, not everybody. Only his friends and the few who are on the inside. There's an ugly story going about privately as to how he got the ambassadorship. They say he was bought with it. But—he's admired and envied even by a good many who know or suspect that he's only an article of commerce. He's got the cash and he's got position; and his paper gives him tremendous power. Then too, as you say, all about him there are men like himself. The only punishment he's likely to get is the penalty of having to live with himself."

"A good, round price if French is not mistaken," replied Saverhill.

The two men passed on. Howard and Marian looked guiltily about, then slipped away in the opposite direction. He helped her into the waiting hansom. As they were driven homeward she cast a stealthy side-glance at him.

"Yes," she thought, "the portrait is a portrait of his face; and his face is a portrait of himself."

He caught her glance in the little mirror in the side of the hansom—caught it and read it. And he began to hate her, this instrument to his punishment, this constant remembrancer of his downfall.

Americans in Fiction

A series of reprints of 19th century American novels important to the study of American folklore, culture and literary history

THOMAS BAILEY ALDRICH
The Stillwater Tragedy

JAMES LANE ALLEN
A Kentucky Cardinal

GERTRUDE ATHERTON
Los Cerritos: A Romance of Modern Times
The Californians
Senator North
Aristocrats
The Splendid Idle Forties

ARLO BATES
The Puritans

OLIVER THOMAS BEARD
Bristling With Thorns

ALICE BROWN
Tiverton Tales
The County Road

FRANCIS H. BURNETT
Through One Administration

WILLIAM A. CARUTHERS
Kentuckian in New York, or the Adventures of Three Southerns
The Cavaliers of Virginia

CHARLES WADDELL CHESNUTT
The Conjure Woman
The Wife of His Youth; and Other Stories of the Colour Line
The House Behind the Cedars

KATE CHOPIN
Bayou Folk

JOHN ESTEN COOKE
The Virginia Comedians
Surry of Eagle's Nest
Mohun: or the Last Days of Lee and His Paladins
My Lady Pokahontas

ROSE TERRY COOKE
Rootbound and Other Sketches

MARGARET DELAND
John Ward, Preacher

THOMAS DIXON
The Leopard's Spots
The Clansman

EDWARD EGGLESTON
Roxy
The Faith Doctor

MARY HALLOCK FOOTE
The Led-Horse Claim

PAUL LEICESTER FORD
The Honorable Peter Stirling

HAROLD FREDERIC
Seth's Brother's Wife

MARY E. WILKINS FREEMAN
A New England Nun; and Other Stories
The Portion of Labor

HENRY B. FULLER
The Cliff Dwellers